The Abysmal Brute

&

Stories of Ships and the Sea

Jack London

The Abysmal Brute & Stories of Ships and the Sea

ISBN: 978-1-64799-424-2

CONTENTS

THE ABYSMAL BRUTE

I

Sam Stubener ran through his mail carelessly and rapidly. As became a manager of prize-fighters, he was accustomed to a various and bizarre correspondence. Every crank, sport, near sport, and reformer seemed to have ideas to impart to him. From dire threats against his life to milder threats, such as pushing in the front of his face, from rabbit-foot fetishes to lucky horse-shoes, from dinky jerkwater bids to the quarter-of-a-million-dollar offers of irresponsible nobodies, he knew the whole run of the surprise portion of his mail. In his time having received a razor-strop made from the skin of a lynched negro, and a finger, withered and sun-dried, cut from the body of a white man found in Death Valley, he was of the opinion that never again would the postman bring him anything that could startle him. But this morning he opened a letter that he read a second time, put away in his pocket, and took out for a third reading. It was postmarked from some unheard-of post-office in Siskiyou County, and it ran:

Dear Sam:

You don't know me, except my reputation. You come after my time, and I've been out of the game a long time. But take it from me I ain't been asleep. I've followed the whole game, and I've followed you, from the time Kal Aufman knocked you out to your last handling of Nat Belson, and I take it you're the niftiest thing in the line of managers that ever came down the pike.

1

I got a proposition for you. I got the greatest unknown that ever happened. This ain't con. It's the straight goods. What do you think of a husky that tips the scales at two hundred and twenty pounds fighting weight, is twenty-two years old, and can hit a kick twice as hard as my best ever? That's him, my boy, Young Pat Glendon, that's the name he'll fight under. I've planned it all out. Now the best thing you can do is hit the first train and come up here.

I bred him and I trained him. All that I ever had in my head I've hammered into his. And maybe you won't believe it, but he's added to it. He's a born fighter. He's a wonder at time and distance. He just knows to the second and the inch, and he don't have to think about it at all. His six-inch jolt is more the real sleep medicine than the full-arm swing of most geezers.

Talk about the hope of the white race. This is him. Come and take a peep. When you was managing Jeffries you was crazy about hunting. Come along and I'll give you some real hunting and fishing that will make your moving picture winnings look like thirty cents. I'll send Young Pat out with you. I ain't able to get around. That's why I'm sending for you. I was going to manage him myself. But it ain't no use. I'm all in and likely to pass out any time. So get a move on. I want you to manage him. There's a fortune in it for both of you, but I want to draw up the contract.

Yours truly,

PAT GLENDON

Stubener was puzzled. It seemed, on the face of it, a joke—the men in the fighting game were notorious jokers—and he tried to discern the fine hand of Corbett or the big friendly paw of Fitzsimmons in the screed before him. But if it were genuine, he knew it was worth looking into. Pat Glendon was before his time, though, as a cub, he had once seen Old Pat spar at the benefit for Jack Dempsey. Even then he was called "Old" Pat, and had been out of the ring for years. He had antedated Sullivan, in the old London Prize Ring Rules, though his last fading battles had been put up under the incoming Marquis of Queensbury Rules.

What ring-follower did not know of Pat Glendon?—though few were alive who had seen him in his prime, and there were not many more who had seen him at all. Yet his name had come down in the history of the ring, and no sporting writer's lexicon was complete without it. His fame was paradoxical. No man was honored higher, and yet he had never attained championship honors. He had been unfortunate, and had been known as the unlucky fighter.

Four times he all but won the heavyweight championship, and each time he had deserved to win it. There was the time on the barge, in San Francisco Bay, when, at the moment he had the champion going, he snapped his own forearm; and on the island in the Thames, sloshing about in six inches of rising tide, he broke a leg at a similar stage in a winning fight; in Texas, too, there was the never-to-be-forgotten day when the police broke in just as he had his man going in all certainty. And finally, there was the fight in the Mechanics' Pavilion in San Francisco, when he was secretly jobbed from the first by a gun-fighting bad man of a referee backed by a small syndicate of bettors. Pat Glendon had had no accidents in that fight, but when he had knocked his man cold with a right to the jaw

3

and a left to the solar plexus, the referee calmly disqualified him for fouling. Every ringside witness, every sporting expert, and the whole sporting world, knew there had been no foul. Yet, like all fighters, Pat Glendon had agreed to abide by the decision of the referee. Pat abided, and accepted it as in keeping with the rest of his bad luck.

This was Pat Glendon. What bothered Stubener was whether or not Pat had written the letter. He carried it down town with him. What's become of Pat Glendon? Such was his greeting to all sports that morning. Nobody seemed to know. Some thought he must be dead, but none knew positively. The fight editor of a morning daily looked up the records and was able to state that his death had not been noted. It was from Tim Donovan, that he got a clue.

"Sure an' he ain't dead," said Donovan. "How could that be?—a man of his make that never boozed or blew himself? He made money, and what's more, he saved it and invested it. Didn't he have three saloons at the one time? An' wasn't he makin' slathers of money with them when he sold out? Now that I'm thinkin', that was the last time I laid eyes on him—when he sold them out. 'Twas all of twenty years and more ago. His wife had just died. I met him headin' for the Ferry. 'Where away, old sport?' says I. 'It's me for the woods,' says he. 'I've quit. Good-by, Tim, me boy.' And I've never seen him from that day to this. Of course he ain't dead."

"You say when his wife died—did he have any children?" Stubener queried.

"One, a little baby. He was luggin' it in his arms that very day."

"Was it a boy?"

"How should I be knowin'?"

4

It was then that Sam Stubener reached a decision, and that night found him in a Pullman speeding toward the wilds of Northern California.

II

Stubener was dropped off the overland at Deer Lick in the early morning, and he kicked his heels for an hour before the one saloon opened its doors. No, the saloonkeeper didn't know anything about Pat Glendon, had never heard of him, and if he was in that part of the country he must be out beyond somewhere. Neither had the one hanger-on ever heard of Pat Glendon. At the hotel the same ignorance obtained, and it was not until the storekeeper and postmaster opened up that Stubener struck the trail. Oh, yes, Pat Glendon lived out beyond. You took the stage at Alpine, which was forty miles and which was a logging camp. From Alpine, on horseback, you rode up Antelope Valley and crossed the divide to Bear Creek. Pat Glendon lived somewhere beyond that. The people of Alpine would know. Yes, there was a young Pat. The storekeeper had seen him. He had been in to Deer Lick two years back. Old Pat had not put in an appearance for five years. He bought his supplies at the store, and always paid by check, and he was a white-haired,

5

strange old man. That was all the storekeeper knew, but the folks at Alpine could give him final directions.

It looked good to Stubener. Beyond doubt there was a young Pat Glendon, as well as an old one, living out beyond. That night the manager spent at the logging camp of Alpine, and early the following morning he rode a mountain cayuse up Antelope Valley. He rode over the divide and down Bear Creek. He rode all day, through the wildest, roughest country he had ever seen, and at sunset turned up Pinto Valley on a trail so stiff and narrow that more than once he elected to get off and walk.

It was eleven o'clock when he dismounted before a log cabin and was greeted by the baying of two huge deer-hounds. Then Pat Glendon opened the door, fell on his neck, and took him in.

"I knew ye'd come, Sam, me boy," said Pat, the while he limped about, building a fire, boiling coffee, and frying a big bear-steak. "The young un ain't home the night. We was gettin' short of meat, and he went out about sundown to pick up a deer. But I'll say no more. Wait till ye see him. He'll be home in the morn, and then you can try him out. There's the gloves. But wait till ye see him.

"As for me, I'm finished. Eighty-one come next January, an' pretty good for an ex-bruiser. But I never wasted meself, Sam, nor kept late hours an' burned the candle at all ends. I had a damned good candle, an' made the most of it, as you'll grant at lookin' at me. And I've taught the same to the young un. What do you think of a lad of twenty-two that's never had a drink in his life nor tasted tobacco? That's him. He's a giant, and he's lived natural all his days. Wait till he takes you out after deer. He'll break your heart travelin' light, him a carryin' the outfit and a big buck deer belike. He's a child of the open air, an' winter nor summer has he slept under a roof. The

6

open for him, as I taught him. The one thing that worries me is how he'll take to sleepin' in houses, an' how he'll stand the tobacco smoke in the ring. 'Tis a terrible thing, that smoke, when you're fighting hard an' gaspin' for air. But no more, Sam, me boy. You're tired an' sure should be sleepin'. Wait till you see him, that's all. Wait till you see him."

But the garrulousness of age was on old Pat, and it was long before he permitted Stubener's eyes to close.

"He can run a deer down with his own legs, that young un," he broke out again. "'Tis the dandy trainin' for the lungs, the hunter's life. He don't know much of else, though, he's read a few books at times an' poetry stuff. He's just plain pure natural, as you'll see when you clap eyes on him. He's got the old Irish strong in him. Sometimes, the way he moons about, it's thinkin' strong I am that he believes in the fairies and such-like. He's a nature lover if ever there was one, an' he's afeard of cities. He's read about them, but the biggest he was ever in was Deer Lick. He misliked the many people, and his report was that they'd stand weedin' out. That was two years agone—the first and the last time he's seen a locomotive and a train of cars.

"Sometimes it's wrong I'm thinkin' I am, bringin' him up a natural. It's given him wind and stamina and the strength o' wild bulls. No city-grown man can have a look-in against him. I'm willin' to grant that Jeffries at his best could 'a' worried the young un a bit, but only a bit. The young un could 'a' broke him like a straw. An' he don't look it. That's the everlasting wonder of it. He's only a fine-seeming young husky; but it's the quality of his muscle that's different. But wait till ye see him, that's all.

"A strange liking the boy has for posies, an' little meadows, a bit of pine with the moon beyond, windy sunsets, or the sun o' morns from the top of old Baldy. An' he has a hankerin' for the drawin' o' pitchers of things, an' of spouting about 'Lucifer or night' from the poetry books he got from the red-headed school teacher. But 'tis only his youngness. He'll settle down to the game once we get him started, but watch out for grouches when it first comes to livin' in a city for him.

"A good thing; he's woman-shy. They'll not bother him for years. He can't bring himself to understand the creatures, an' damn few of them has he seen at that. 'Twas the school teacher over at Samson's Flat that put the poetry stuff in his head. She was clean daffy over the young un, an' he never a-knowin'. A warm-haired girl she was—not a mountain girl, but from down in the flat-lands—an' as time went by she was fair desperate, an' the way she went after him was shameless. An' what d'ye think the boy did when he tumbled to it? He was scared as a jackrabbit. He took blankets an' ammunition an' hiked for tall timber. Not for a month did I lay eyes on him, an' then he sneaked in after dark and was gone in the morn. Nor would he as much as peep at her letters. 'Burn 'em,' he said. An' burn 'em I did. Twice she rode over on a cayuse all the way from Samson's Flat, an' I was sorry for the young creature. She was fair hungry for the boy, and she looked it in her face. An' at the end of three months she gave up school an' went back to her own country, an' then it was that the boy came home to the shack to live again.

"Women ha' ben the ruination of many a good fighter, but they won't be of him. He blushes like a girl if anything young in skirts looks at him a second time or too long the first one. An' they all look at him. But when he fights, when he fights!—God! it's the old savage Irish that flares in him, an' drives the fists of. Not that he

8

goes off his base. Don't walk away with that. At my best I was never as cool as he. I misdoubt 'twas the wrath of me that brought the accidents. But he's an iceberg. He's hot an' cold at the one time, a live wire in an ice-chest."

Stubener was dozing, when the old man's mumble aroused him. He listened drowsily.

"I made a man o' him, by God! I made a man o' him, with the two fists of him, an' the upstanding legs of him, an' the straight-seein' eyes. And I know the game in my head, an' I've kept up with the times and the modern changes. The crouch? Sure, he knows all the styles an' economies. He never moves two inches when an inch and a half will do the turn. And when he wants he can spring like a buck kangaroo. In-fightin'? Wait till you see. Better than his out-fightin', and he could sure 'a' sparred with Peter Jackson an' outfooted Corbett in his best. I tell you, I've taught'm it all, to the last trick, and he's improved on the teachin'. He's a fair genius at the game. An' he's had plenty of husky mountain men to try out on. I gave him the fancy work and they gave him the sloggin'. Nothing shy or delicate about them. Roarin' bulls an' big grizzly bears, that's what they are, when it comes to huggin' in a clinch or swingin' rough-like in the rushes. An' he plays with 'em. Man, d'ye hear me?—he plays with them, like you an' me would play with little puppy-dogs."

Another time Stubener awoke, to hear the old man mumbling:

"'Tis the funny think he don't take fightin' seriously. It's that easy to him he thinks it play. But wait till he's tapped a swift one. That's all, wait. An' you'll see'm throw on the juice in that cold storage plant of his an' turn loose the prettiest scientific wallopin' that ever you laid eyes on."

In the shivery gray of mountain dawn, Stubener was routed from his blankets by old Pat.

"He's comin' up the trail now," was the hoarse whisper. "Out with ye an' take your first peep at the biggest fightin' man the ring has ever seen, or will ever see in a thousand years again."

The manager peered through the open door, rubbing the sleep from his heavy eyes, and saw a young giant walk into the clearing. In one hand was a rifle, across his shoulders a heavy deer under which he moved as if it were weightless. He was dressed roughly in blue overalls and woolen shirt open at the throat. Coat he had none, and on his feet, instead of brogans, were moccasins. Stubener noted that his walk was smooth and catlike, without suggestion of his two hundred and twenty pounds of weight to which that of the deer was added. The fight manager was impressed from the first glimpse. Formidable the young fellow certainly was, but the manager sensed the strangeness and unusualness of him. He was a new type, something different from the run of fighters. He seemed a creature of the wild, more a night-roaming figure from some old fairy story or folk tale than a twentieth-century youth.

A thing Stubener quickly discovered was that young Pat was not much of a talker. He acknowledged old Pat's introduction with a grip of the hand but without speech, and silently set to work at building the fire and getting breakfast. To his father's direct questions he answered in monosyllables, as, for instance, when asked where he had picked up the deer.

"South Fork," was all he vouchsafed.

"Eleven miles across the mountains," the old man exposited pridefully to Stubener, "an' a trail that'd break your heart."

Breakfast consisted of black coffee, sourdough bread, and an immense quantity of bear-meat broiled over the coals. Of this the young fellow ate ravenously, and Stubener divined that both the Glendons were accustomed to an almost straight meat diet. Old Pat did all the talking, though it was not till the meal was ended that he broached the subject he had at heart.

"Pat, boy," he began, "you know who the gentleman is?"

Young Pat nodded, and cast a quick, comprehensive glance at the manager.

"Well, he'll be takin' you away with him and down to San Francisco."

"I'd sooner stay here, dad," was the answer.

Stubener felt a prick of disappointment. It was a wild goose chase after all. This was no fighter, eager and fretting to be at it. His huge brawn counted for nothing. It was nothing new. It was the big fellows that usually had the streak of fat.

But old Pat's Celtic wrath flared up, and his voice was harsh with command.

"You'll go down to the cities an' fight, me boy. That's what I've trained you for, an' you'll do it."

"All right," was the unexpected response, rumbled apathetically from the deep chest.

"And fight like hell," the old man added.

Again Stubener felt disappointment at the absence of flash and fire in the young man's eyes as he answered:

11

"All right. When do we start?"

"Oh, Sam, here, he'll be wantin' a little huntin' and to fish a bit, as well as to try you out with the gloves." He looked at Sam, who nodded. "Suppose you strip and give'm a taste of your quality."

An hour later, Sam Stubener had his eyes opened. An ex-fighter himself, a heavyweight at that, he was even a better judge of fighters, and never had he seen one strip to like advantage.

"See the softness of him," old Pat chanted. "'Tis the true stuff. Look at the slope of the shoulders, an' the lungs of him. Clean, all clean, to the last drop an' ounce of him. You're lookin' at a man, Sam, the like of which was never seen before. Not a muscle of him bound. No weight-lifter or Sandow exercise artist there. See the fat snakes of muscles a-crawlin' soft an' lazy-like. Wait till you see them flashin' like a strikin' rattler. He's good for forty rounds this blessed instant, or a hundred. Go to it! Time!"

They went to it, for three-minute rounds with a minute rests, and Sam Stubener was immediately undeceived. Here was no streak of fat, no apathy, only a lazy, good-natured play of gloves and tricks, with a brusk stiffness and harsh sharpness in the contacts that he knew belonged only to the trained and instinctive fighting man.

"Easy, now, easy," old Pat warned. "Sam's not the man he used to be."

This nettled Sam, as it was intended to do, and he played his most famous trick and favorite punch—a feint for a clinch and a right rip to the stomach. But, quickly as it was delivered, young Pat saw it, and, though it landed, his body was going away. The next time, his body did not go away. As the rip started, he moved forward and twisted his left hip to meet it. It was only a matter of several inches, yet it blocked the blow. And thereafter, try as he would, Stubener's glove got no farther than that hip.

Stubener had roughed it with big men in his time, and, in exhibition bouts, had creditably held his own. But there was no holding his own here. Young Pat played with him, and in the clinches made him feel as powerful as a baby, landing on him seemingly at will, locking and blocking with masterful accuracy, and scarcely noticing or acknowledging his existence. Half the time young Pat seemed to spend in gazing off and out at the landscape in a dreamy sort of way. And right here Stubener made another mistake. He took it for a trick of old Pat's training, tried to sneak in a short-arm jolt, found his arm in a lightning lock, and had both his ears cuffed for his pains.

"The instinct for a blow," the old man chortled. "'Tis not put on, I'm tellin' you. He is a wiz. He knows a blow without the lookin', when it starts an' where, the speed, an' space, an' niceness of it. An' 'tis nothing I ever showed him. 'Tis inspiration. He was so born."

Once, in a clinch, the fight manager heeled his glove on young Pat's mouth, and there was just a hint of viciousness in the manner of doing it. A moment later, in the next clinch, Sam received the heel of the other's glove on his own mouth. There was nothing snappy about it, but the pressure, stolidly lazy as it was, put his head back till the joints cracked and for the moment he thought his neck was broken. He slacked his body and dropped his arms in token that the bout was over, felt the instant release, and staggered clear.

"He'll—he'll do," he gasped, looking the admiration he lacked the breath to utter.

Old Pat's eyes were brightly moist with pride and triumph.

"An' what will you be thinkin' to happen when some of the gay an' ugly ones tries to rough it on him?" he asked.

"He'll kill them, sure," was Stubener's verdict.

"No; he's too cool for that. But he'll just hurt them some for their dirtiness."

"Let's draw up the contract," said the manager.

"Wait till you know the whole worth of him!" Old Pat answered. "'Tis strong terms I'll be makin' you come to. Go for a deer-hunt with the boy over the hills an' learn the lungs and the legs of him. Then we'll sign up iron-clad and regular."

Stubener was gone two days on that hunt, and he learned all and more than old Pat had promised, and came back a very weary and very humble man. The young fellow's innocence of the world had been startling to the case-hardened manager, but he had found him nobody's fool. Virgin though his mind was, untouched by all save a narrow mountain experience, nevertheless he had proved possession of a natural keenness and shrewdness far beyond the average. In a way he was a mystery to Sam, who could not understand his terrible equanimity of temper. Nothing ruffled him or worried him, and his patience was of an enduring primitiveness. He never swore, not even the futile and emasculated cuss-words of sissy-boys.

"I'd swear all right if I wanted to," he had explained, when challenged by his companion. "But I guess I've never come to needing it. When I do, I'll swear, I suppose."

Old Pat, resolutely adhering to his decision, said good-by at the cabin.

14

"It won't be long, Pat, boy, when I'll be readin' about you in the papers. I'd like to go along, but I'm afeard it's me for the mountains till the end."

And then, drawing the manager aside, the old man turned loose on him almost savagely.

"Remember what I've ben tellin' ye over an' over. The boy's clean an' he's honest. He knows nothing of the rottenness of the game. I kept it all away from him, I tell you. He don't know the meanin' of fake. He knows only the bravery, an' romance an' glory of fightin', and I've filled him up with tales of the old ring heroes, though little enough, God knows, it's set him afire. Man, man, I'm tellin' you that I clipped the fight columns from the newspapers to keep it 'way from him—him a-thinkin' I was wantin' them for me scrap book. He don't know a man ever lay down or threw a fight. So don't you get him in anything that ain't straight. Don't turn the boy's stomach. That's why I put in the null and void clause. The first rottenness and the contract's broke of itself. No snide division of stake-money; no secret arrangements with the movin' pitcher men for guaranteed distance. There's slathers o' money for the both of you. But play it square or you lose. Understand?

"And whatever you'll be doin' watch out for the women," was old Pat's parting admonishment, young Pat astride his horse and reining in dutifully to hear. "Women is death an' damnation, remember that. But when you do find the one, the only one, hang on to her. She'll be worth more than glory an' money. But first be sure, an' when you're sure, don't let her slip through your fingers. Grab her with the two hands of you and hang on. Hang on if all the world goes to smash an' smithereens. Pat, boy, a good woman is … a good woman. 'Tis the first word and the last."

15

III

Once in San Francisco, Sam Stubener's troubles began. Not that young Pat had a nasty temper, or was grouchy as his father had feared. On the contrary, he was phenomenally sweet and mild. But he was homesick for his beloved mountains. Also, he was secretly appalled by the city, though he trod its roaring streets imperturbable as a red Indian.

"I came down here to fight," he announced, at the end of the first week.

"Where's Jim Hanford?"

Stubener whistled.

"A big champion like him wouldn't look at you," was his answer. "'Go and get a reputation,' is what he'd say."

"I can lick him."

"But the public doesn't know that. If you licked him you'd be champion of the world, and no champion ever became so with his first fight."

"I can."

"But the public doesn't know it, Pat. It wouldn't come to see you fight. And it's the crowd that brings the money and the big purses. That's why Jim Hanford wouldn't consider you for a second. There'd be nothing in it for him. Besides, he's getting three thousand a week right now in vaudeville, with a contract for twenty-five weeks. Do you think he'd chuck that for a go with a man no one ever heard of? You've got to do something first, make a

16

record. You've got to begin on the little local dubs that nobody ever heard of—guys like Chub Collins, Rough-House Kelly, and the Flying Dutchman. When you've put them away, you're only started on the first round of the ladder. But after that you'll go up like a balloon."

"I'll meet those three named in the same ring one after the other," was Pat's decision. "Make the arrangements accordingly."

Stubener laughed.

"What's wrong? Don't you think I can put them away?"

"I know you can," Stubener assured him. "But it can't be arranged that way. You've got to take them one at a time. Besides, remember, I know the game and I'm managing you. This proposition has to be worked up, and I'm the boy that knows how. If we're lucky, you may get to the top in a couple of years and be the champion with a mint of money."

Pat sighed at the prospect, then brightened up.

"And after that I can retire and go back home to the old man," he said.

Stubener was about to reply, but checked himself. Strange as was this championship material, he felt confident that when the top was reached it would prove very similar to that of all the others who had gone before. Besides, two years was a long way off, and there was much to be done in the meantime.

When Pat fell to moping around his quarters, reading endless poetry books and novels drawn from the public library, Stubener sent him off to live on a Contra Costa ranch across the Bay, under the watchful eye of Spider Walsh. At the end of a week Spider

17

whispered that the job was a cinch. His charge was away and over the hills from dawn till dark, whipping the streams for trout, shooting quail and rabbits, and pursuing the one lone and crafty buck famous for having survived a decade of hunters. It was the Spider who waxed lazy and fat, while his charge kept himself in condition.

As Stubener expected, his unknown was laughed at by the fight club managers. Were not the woods full of unknowns who were always breaking out with championship rashes? A preliminary, say of four rounds—yes, they would grant him that. But the main event—never. Stubener was resolved that young Pat should make his debut in nothing less than a main event, and, by the prestige of his own name he at last managed it. With much misgiving, the Mission Club agreed that Pat Glendon could go fifteen rounds with Rough-House Kelly for a purse of one hundred dollars. It was the custom of young fighters to assume the names of old ring heroes, so no one suspected that he was the son of the great Pat Glendon, while Stubener held his peace. It was a good press surprise package to spring later.

Came the night of the fight, after a month of waiting. Stubener's anxiety was keen. His professional reputation was staked that his man would make a showing, and he was astounded to see Pat, seated in his corner a bare five minutes, lose the healthy color from his cheeks, which turned a sickly yellow.

"Cheer up, boy," Stubener said, slapping him on the shoulder. "The first time in the ring is always strange, and Kelly has a way of letting his opponent wait for him on the chance of getting stage-fright."

"It isn't that," Pat answered. "It's the tobacco smoke. I'm not used to it, and it's making me fair sick."

18

His manager experienced the quick shock of relief. A man who turned sick from mental causes, even if he were a Samson, could never win to place in the prize ring. As for tobacco smoke, the youngster would have to get used to it, that was all.

Young Pat's entrance into the ring had been met with silence, but when Rough-House Kelly crawled through the ropes his greeting was uproarious. He did not belie his name. He was a ferocious-looking man, black and hairy, with huge, knotty muscles, weighing a full two hundred pounds. Pat looked across at him curiously, and received a savage scowl. After both had been introduced to the audience, they shook hands. And even as their gloves gripped, Kelly ground his teeth, convulsed his face with an expression of rage, and muttered:

"You've got yer nerve wid yeh." He flung Pat's hand roughly from his, and hissed, "I'll eat yeh up, ye pup!"

The audience laughed at the action, and it guessed hilariously at what Kelly must have said.

Back in his corner, and waiting the gong, Pat turned to Stubener.

"Why is he angry with me?" he asked.

"He ain't," Stubener answered. "That's his way, trying to scare you. It's just mouth-fighting."

"It isn't boxing," was Pat's comment; and Stubener, with a quick glance, noted that his eyes were as mildly blue as ever.

"Be careful," the manager warned, as the gong for the first round sounded and Pat stood up. "He's liable to come at you like a man-eater."

19

And like a man-eater Kelly did come at him, rushing across the ring in wild fury. Pat, who in his easy way had advanced only a couple of paces, gauged the other's momentum, side-stepped, and brought his stiff-arched right across to the jaw. Then he stood and looked on with a great curiosity. The fight was over. Kelly had fallen like a stricken bullock to the floor, and there he lay without movement while the referee, bending over him, shouted the ten seconds in his unheeding ear. When Kelly's seconds came to lift him, Pat was before them. Gathering the huge, inert bulk of the man in his arms, he carried him to his corner and deposited him on the stool and in the arms of his seconds.

Half a minute later, Kelly's head lifted and his eyes wavered open. He looked about him stupidly and then to one of his seconds.

"What happened?" he queried hoarsely. "Did the roof fall on me?"

IV

As a result of his fight with Kelly, though the general opinion was that he had won by a fluke, Pat was matched with Rufe Mason. This took place three weeks later, and the Sierra Club audience at Dreamland Rink failed to see what happened. Rufe Mason was a heavyweight, noted locally for his cleverness. When the gong for

20

the first round sounded, both men met in the center of the ring. Neither rushed. Nor did they strike a blow. They felt around each other, their arms bent, their gloves so close together that they almost touched. This lasted for perhaps five seconds. Then it happened, and so quickly that not one in a hundred of the audience saw. Rufe Mason made a feint with his right. It was obviously not a real feint, but a feeler, a mere tentative threatening of a possible blow. It was at this instant that Pat loosed his punch. So close together were they that the distance the blow traveled was a scant eight inches. It was a short-arm left jolt, and it was accomplished by a twist of the left forearm and a thrust of the shoulder. It landed flush on the point of the chin and the astounded audience saw Rufe Mason's legs crumple under him as his body sank to the floor. But the referee had seen, and he promptly proceeded to count him out. Again Pat carried his opponent to his corner, and it was ten minutes before Rufe Mason, supported by his seconds, with sagging knees and rolling, glassy eyes, was able to move down the aisle through the stupefied and incredulous audience on the way to his dressing room.

"No wonder," he told a reporter, "that Rough-House Kelly thought the roof hit him."

After Chub Collins had been put out in the twelfth second of the first round of a fifteen-round contest, Stubener felt compelled to speak to Pat.

"Do you know what they're calling you now?" he asked.

Pat shook his head.

"One Punch Glendon."

Pat smiled politely. He was little interested in what he was called.

21

He had certain work cut out which he must do ere he could win back to his mountains, and he was phlegmatically doing it, that was all.

"It won't do," his manager continued, with an ominous shake of the head. "You can't go on putting your men out so quickly. You must give them more time."

"I'm here to fight, ain't I?" Pat demanded in surprise.

Again Stubener shook his head.

"It's this way, Pat. You've got to be big and generous in the fighting game. Don't get all the other fighters sore. And it's not fair to the audience. They want a run for their money. Besides, no one will fight you. They'll all be scared out. And you can't draw crowds with ten-second fights. I leave it to you. Would you pay a dollar, or five, to see a ten-second fight?"

Pat was convinced, and he promised to give future audiences the requisite run for their money, though he stated that, personally, he preferred going fishing to witnessing a hundred rounds of fighting.

And still, Pat had got practically nowhere in the game. The local sports laughed when his name was mentioned. It called to mind funny fights and Rough-House Kelly's remark about the roof. Nobody knew how Pat could fight. They had never seen him. Where was his wind, his stamina, his ability to mix it with rough customers through long grueling contests? He had demonstrated nothing but the possession of a lucky punch and a depressing proclivity for flukes.

So it was that his fourth match was arranged with Pete Sosso, a Portuguese fighter from Butchertown, known only for the amazing tricks he played in the ring. Pat did not train for the fight. Instead he made a flying and sorrowful trip to the mountains to bury his father. Old Pat had known well the condition of his heart, and it had stopped suddenly on him.

Young Pat arrived back in San Francisco with so close a margin of time that he changed into his fighting togs directly from his traveling suit, and even then the audience was kept waiting ten minutes.

"Remember, give him a chance," Stubener cautioned him as he climbed through the ropes. "Play with him, but do it seriously. Let him go ten or twelve rounds, then get him."

Pat obeyed instructions, and, though it would have been easy enough to put Sosso out, so tricky was he that to stand up to him and not put him out kept his hands full. It was a pretty exhibition, and the audience was delighted. Sosso's whirlwind attacks, wild feints, retreats, and rushes, required all Pat's science to protect himself, and even then he did not escape unscathed.

Stubener praised him in the minute-rests, and all would have been well, had not Sosso, in the fourth round, played one of his most spectacular tricks. Pat, in a mix-up, had landed a hook to Sosso's jaw, when to his amazement, the latter dropped his hands and reeled backward, eyes rolling, legs bending and giving, in a high state of grogginess. Pat could not understand. It had not been a knock-out blow, and yet there was his man all ready to fall to the mat. Pat dropped his own hands and wonderingly watched his reeling opponent. Sosso staggered away, almost fell, recovered, and staggered obliquely and blindly forward again.

For the first and the last time in his fighting career, Pat was caught

23

off his guard. He actually stepped aside to let the reeling man go by. Still reeling, Sosso suddenly loosed his right. Pat received it full on his jaw with an impact that rattled all his teeth. A great roar of delight went up from the audience. But Pat did not hear. He saw only Sosso before him, grinning and defiant, and not the least bit groggy. Pat was hurt by the blow, but vastly more outraged by the trick. All the wrath that his father ever had surged up in him. He shook his head as if to get rid of the shock of the blow and steadied himself before his man. It all occurred in the next second. With a feint that drew his opponent, Pat fetched his left to the solar plexus, almost at the same instant whipping his right across to the jaw. The latter blow landed on Sosso's mouth ere his falling body struck the floor. The club doctors worked half an hour to bring him to. After that they put eleven stitches in his mouth and packed him off in an ambulance.

"I'm sorry," Pat told his manager, "I'm afraid I lost my temper. I'll never do it again in the ring. Dad always cautioned me about it. He said it had made him lose more than one battle. I didn't know I could lose my temper that way, but now that I know I'll keep it in control."

And Stubener believed him. He was coming to the stage where he could believe anything about his young charge.

"You don't need to get angry," he said, "you're so thoroughly the master of your man at any stage."

"At any inch or second of the fight," Pat affirmed.

"And you can put them out any time you want."

"Sure I can. I don't want to boast. But I just seem to possess the ability. My eyes show me the opening that my skill knows how to

24

make, and time and distance are second nature to me. Dad called it a gift, but I thought he was blarneying me. Now that I've been up against these men, I guess he was right. He said I had the mind and muscle correlation."

"At any inch or second of the fight," Stubener repeated musingly.

Pat nodded, and Stubener, absolutely believing him, caught a vision of a golden future that should have fetched old Pat out of his grave.

"Well, don't forget, we've got to give the crowd a run for its money," he said. "We'll fix it up between us how many rounds a fight should go. Now your next bout will be with the Flying Dutchman. Suppose you let it run the full fifteen and put him out in the last round. That will give you a chance to make a showing as well."

"All right, Sam," was the answer.

"It will be a test for you," Stubener warned. "You may fail to put him out in that last round."

"Watch me." Pat paused to put weight to his promise, and picked up a volume of Longfellow. "If I don't I'll never read poetry again, and that's going some."

"You bet it is," his manager proclaimed jubilantly, "though what you see in such stuff is beyond me."

Pat sighed, but did not reply. In all his life he had found but one person who cared for poetry, and that had been the red-haired school teacher who scared him off into the woods.

V

"Where are you going?" Stubener demanded in surprise, looking at his watch.

Pat, with his hand on the door-knob, paused and turned around.

"To the Academy of Sciences," he said. "There's a professor who's going to give a lecture there on Browning to-night, and Browning is the sort of writer you need assistance with. Sometimes I think I ought to go to night school."

"But great Scott, man!" exclaimed the horrified manager. "You're on with the Flying Dutchman to-night."

"I know it. But I won't enter the ring a moment before half past nine or quarter to ten. The lecture will be over at nine fifteen. If you want to make sure, come around and pick me up in your machine."

Stubener shrugged his shoulders helplessly.

"You've got no kick coming," Pat assured him. "Dad used to tell me a man's worst time was in the hours just before a fight, and that many a fight was lost by a man's breaking down right there, with nothing to do but think and be anxious. Well, you'll never need to worry about me that way. You ought to be glad I can go off to a lecture."

And later that night, in the course of watching fifteen splendid rounds, Stubener chuckled to himself more than once at the idea of what that audience of sports would think, did it know that this magnificent young prize-fighter had come to the ring directly from a Browning lecture.

26

The Flying Dutchman was a young Swede who possessed an unwonted willingness to fight and who was blessed with phenomenal endurance. He never rested, was always on the offensive, and rushed and fought from gong to gong. In the out-fighting his arms whirled about like flails, in the in-fighting he was forever shouldering or half-wrestling and starting blows whenever he could get a hand free. From start to finish he was a whirlwind, hence his name. His failing was lack of judgment in time and distance. Nevertheless he had won many fights by virtue of landing one in each dozen or so of the unending fusillades of punches he delivered. Pat, with strong upon him the caution that he must not put his opponent out, was kept busy. Nor, though he escaped vital damage, could he avoid entirely those eternal flying gloves. But it was good training, and in a mild way he enjoyed the contest.

"Could you get him now?" Stubener whispered in his ear during the minute rest at the end of the fifth round.

"Sure," was Pat's answer.

"You know he's never yet been knocked out by any one," Stubener warned a couple of rounds later.

"Then I'm afraid I'll have to break my knuckles," Pat smiled. "I know the punch I've got in me, and when I land it something's got to go. If he won't, my knuckles will."

"Do you think you could get him now?" Stubener asked at the end of the thirteenth round.

"Anytime, I tell you."

"Well, then, Pat, let him run to the fifteenth."

In the fourteenth round the Flying Dutchman exceeded himself. At the stroke of the gong he rushed clear across the ring to the opposite corner where Pat was leisurely getting to his feet. The house cheered, for it knew the Flying Dutchman had cut loose. Pat, catching the fun of it, whimsically decided to meet the terrific onslaught with a wholly passive defense and not to strike a blow. Nor did he strike a blow, nor feint a blow, during the three minutes of whirlwind that followed. He gave a rare exhibition of stalling, sometimes hugging his bowed face with his left arm, his abdomen with his right; at other times, changing as the point of attack changed, so that both gloves were held on either side his face, or both elbows and forearms guarded his mid-section; and all the time moving about, clumsily shouldering, or half-falling forward against his opponent and clogging his efforts; himself never striking nor threatening to strike, the while rocking with the impacts of the storming blows that beat upon his various guards the devil's own tattoo.

Those close at the ringside saw and appreciated, but the rest of the audience, fooled, arose to its feet and roared its applause in the mistaken notion that Pat, helpless, was receiving a terrible beating. With the end of the round, the audience, dumbfounded, sank back into its seats as Pat walked steadily to his corner. It was not understandable. He should have been beaten to a pulp, and yet nothing had happened to him.

"Now are you going to get him?" Stubener queried anxiously.

"Inside ten seconds," was Pat's confident assertion. "Watch me."

There was no trick about it. When the gong struck and Pat bounded to his feet, he advertised it unmistakably that for the first time in the fight he was starting after his man. Not one onlooker misunderstood. The Flying Dutchman read the advertisement, too, and for the first time in his career, as they met in the center of the ring, visibly hesitated. For the fraction of a second they faced each other in position. Then the Flying Dutchman leaped forward upon his man, and Pat, with a timed right-cross, dropped him cold as he leaped.

It was after this battle that Pat Glendon started on his upward rush to fame. The sports and the sporting writers took him up. For the first time the Flying Dutchman had been knocked out. His conqueror had proved a wizard of defense. His previous victories had not been flukes. He had a kick in both his hands. Giant that he was, he would go far. The time was already past, the writers asserted, for him to waste himself on the third-raters and chopping blocks. Where were Ben Menzies, Rege Rede, Bill Tarwater, and Ernest Lawson? It was time for them to meet this young cub that had suddenly shown himself a fighter of quality. Where was his manager anyway, that he was not issuing the challenges?

And then fame came in a day; for Stubener divulged the secret that his man was none other than the son of Pat Glendon, Old Pat, the old-time ring hero. "Young" Pat Glendon, he was promptly christened, and sports and writers flocked about him to admire him, and back him, and write him up.

Beginning with Ben Menzies and finishing with Bill Tarwater, he challenged, fought, and knocked out the four second-raters. To do this, he was compelled to travel, the battles taking place in Goldfield, Denver, Texas, and New York. To accomplish it required months, for the bigger fights were not easily arranged, and the men themselves demanded more time for training.

The second year saw him running to cover and disposing of the half-dozen big fighters that clustered just beneath the top of the

29

heavyweight ladder. On this top, firmly planted, stood "Big" Jim Hanford, the undefeated world champion. Here, on the top rungs, progress was slower, though Stubener was indefatigable in issuing challenges and in promoting sporting opinion to force the man to fight. Will King was disposed of in England, and Glendon pursued Tom Harrison half way around the world to defeat him on Boxing Day in Australia.

But the purses grew larger and larger. In place of a hundred dollars, such as his first battles had earned him, he was now receiving from twenty to thirty thousand dollars a fight, as well as equally large sums from the moving picture men. Stubener took his manager's percentage of all this, according to the terms of the contract old Pat had drawn up, and both he and Glendon, despite their heavy expenses, were waxing rich. This was due, more than anything else, to the clean lives they lived. They were not wasters.

Stubener was attracted to real estate, and his holdings in San Francisco, consisting of building flats and apartment houses, were bigger than Glendon ever dreamed. There was a secret syndicate of bettors, however, which could have made an accurate guess at the size of Stubener's holdings, while heavy bonus after heavy bonus, of which Glendon never heard, was paid over to his manager by the moving picture men.

Stubener's most serious task was in maintaining the innocence of his young gladiator. Nor did he find it difficult. Glendon, who had nothing to do with the business end, was little interested. Besides, wherever his travels took him, he spent his spare time in hunting and fishing. He rarely mingled with those of the sporting world, was notoriously shy and secluded, and preferred art galleries and books of verse to sporting gossip. Also, his trainers and sparring partners were rigorously instructed by the manager to keep their tongues away from the slightest hints of ring rottenness. In every way Stubener intervened between Glendon and the world. He was never even interviewed save in Stubener's presence.

Only once was Glendon approached. It was just prior to his battle with Henderson, and an offer of a hundred thousand was made to him to throw the fight. It was made hurriedly, in swift whispers, in a hotel corridor, and it was fortunate for the man that Pat controlled his temper and shouldered past him without reply. He brought the tale of it to Stubener, who said:

"It's only con, Pat. They were trying to josh you." He noted the blue eyes blaze. "And maybe worse than that. If they could have got you to fall for it, there might have been a big sensation in the papers that would have finished you. But I doubt it. Such things don't happen any more. It's a myth, that's what it is, that has come down from the middle history of the ring. There has been rottenness in the past, but no fighter or manager of reputation would dare anything of the sort to-day. Why, Pat, the men in the game are as clean and straight as those in professional baseball, than which there is nothing cleaner or straighter."

And all the while he talked, Stubener knew in his heart that the forthcoming fight with Henderson was not to be shorter than twelve rounds—this for the moving pictures—and not longer than the fourteenth round. And he knew, furthermore, so big were the stakes involved, that Henderson himself was pledged not to last beyond the fourteenth.

And Glendon, never approached again, dismissed the matter from his mind and went out to spend the afternoon in taking color photographs. The camera had become his latest hobby. Loving pictures, yet unable to paint, he had compromised by taking up

31

photography. In his hand baggage was one grip packed with books on the subject, and he spent long hours in the dark room, realizing for himself the various processes. Never had there been a great fighter who was as aloof from the fighting world as he. Because he had little to say with those he encountered, he was called sullen and unsocial, and out of this a newspaper reputation took form that was not an exaggeration so much as it was an entire misconception. Boiled down, his character in print was that of an ox-muscled and dumbly stupid brute, and one callow sporting writer dubbed him the "abysmal brute." The name stuck. The rest of the fraternity hailed it with delight, and thereafter Glendon's name never appeared in print unconnected with it. Often, in a headline or under a photograph, "The Abysmal Brute," capitalized and without quotation marks, appeared alone. All the world knew who was this brute. This made him draw into himself closer than ever, while it developed a bitter prejudice against newspaper folk.

Regarding fighting itself, his earlier mild interest grew stronger. The men he now fought were anything but dubs, and victory did not come so easily. They were picked men, experienced ring generals, and each battle was a problem. There were occasions when he found it impossible to put them out in any designated later round of a fight. Thus, with Sulzberger, the gigantic German, try as he would in the eighteenth round, he failed to get him, in the nineteenth it was the same story, and not till the twentieth did he manage to break through the baffling guard and drop him. Glendon's increasing enjoyment of the game was accompanied by severer and prolonged training. Never dissipating, spending much of his time on hunting trips in the hills, he was practically always in the pink of condition, and, unlike his father, no unfortunate accidents marred his career. He never broke a bone, nor injured so much as a knuckle. One thing that Stubener noted with secret glee was that his young fighter no longer talked of going permanently back to his mountains when he had won the championship away from Jim Hanford.

VI

The consummation of his career was rapidly approaching. The great champion had even publicly intimated his readiness to take on Glendon as soon as the latter had disposed of the three or four aspirants for the championship who intervened. In six months Pat managed to put away Kid McGrath and Philadelphia Jack McBride, and there remained only Nat Powers and Tom Cannam. And all would have been well had not a certain society girl gone adventuring into journalism, and had not Stubener agreed to an interview with the woman reporter of the San Francisco "Courier-Journal."

Her work was always published over the name of Maud Sangster, which, by the way, was her own name. The Sangsters were a notoriously wealthy family. The founder, old Jacob Sangster, had packed his blankets and worked as a farm-hand in the West. He had discovered an inexhaustible borax deposit in Nevada, and, from hauling it out by mule-teams, had built a railroad to do the

33

freighting. Following that, he had poured the profits of borax into the purchase of hundreds and thousands of square miles of timber lands in California, Oregon, and Washington. Still later, he had combined politics with business, bought statesmen, judges, and machines, and become a captain of complicated industry. And after that he had died, full of honor and pessimism, leaving his name a muddy blot for future historians to smudge, and also leaving a matter of a couple of hundreds of millions for his four sons to squabble over. The legal, industrial, and political battles that followed, vexed and amused California for a generation, and culminated in deadly hatred and unspeaking terms between the four sons. The youngest, Theodore, in middle life experienced a change of heart, sold out his stock farms and racing stables, and plunged into a fight with all the corrupt powers of his native state, including most of its millionaires, in a quixotic attempt to purge it of the infamy which had been implanted by old Jacob Sangster.

Maud Sangster was Theodore's oldest daughter. The Sangster stock uniformly bred fighters among the men and beauties among the women. Nor was Maud an exception. Also, she must have inherited some of the virus of adventure from the Sangster breed, for she had come to womanhood and done a multitude of things of which no woman in her position should have been guilty. A match in ten thousand, she remained unmarried. She had sojourned in Europe without bringing home a nobleman for spouse, and had declined a goodly portion of her own set at home. She had gone in for outdoor sports, won the tennis championship of the state, kept the society weeklies agog with her unconventionalities, walked from San Mateo to Santa Cruz against time on a wager, and once caused a sensation by playing polo in a men's team at a private Burlingame practice game. Incidentally, she had gone in for art, and maintained a studio in San Francisco's Latin Quarter.

All this had been of little moment until her father's reform attack became acute. Passionately independent, never yet having met the man to whom she could gladly submit, and bored by those who had aspired, she resented her father's interference with her way of life and put the climax on all her social misdeeds by leaving home and going to work on the "Courier-Journal." Beginning at twenty dollars a week, her salary had swiftly risen to fifty. Her work was principally musical, dramatic, and art criticism, though she was not above mere journalistic stunts if they promised to be sufficiently interesting. Thus she scooped the big interview with Morgan at a time when he was being futilely trailed by a dozen New York star journalists, went down to the bottom of the Golden Gate in a diver's suit, and flew with Rood, the bird man, when he broke all records of continuous flight by reaching as far as Riverside.

Now it must not be imagined that Maud Sangster was a hard-bitten Amazon. On the contrary, she was a gray-eyed, slender young woman, of three or four and twenty, of medium stature, and possessing uncommonly small hands and feet for an outdoor woman or any other kind of a woman. Also, far in excess of most outdoor women, she knew how to be daintily feminine.

It was on her own suggestion that she received the editor's commission to interview Pat Glendon. With the exception of having caught a glimpse, once, of Bob Fitzsimmons in evening dress at the Palace Grill, she had never seen a prizefighter in her life. Nor was she curious to see one—at least she had not been curious until Young Pat Glendon came to San Francisco to train for his fight with Nat Powers. Then his newspaper reputation had aroused her. The Abysmal Brute!—it certainly must be worth seeing. From what she read of him she gleaned that he was a man-monster, profoundly stupid and with the sullenness and ferocity of a jungle beast. True,

35

his published photographs did not show all that, but they did show the hugeness of brawn that might be expected to go with it. And so, accompanied by a staff photographer, she went out to the training quarters at the Cliff House at the hour appointed by Stubener.

That real estate owner was having trouble. Pat was rebellious. He sat, one big leg dangling over the side of the arm chair and Shakespeare's Sonnets face downward on his knee, orating against the new woman.

"What do they want to come butting into the game for?" he demanded. "It's not their place. What do they know about it anyway? The men are bad enough as it is. I'm not a holy show. This woman's coming here to make me one. I never have stood for women around the training quarters, and I don't care if she is a reporter."

"But she's not an ordinary reporter," Stubener interposed. "You've heard of the Sangsters?—the millionaires?"

Pat nodded.

"Well, she's one of them. She's high society and all that stuff. She could be running with the Blingum crowd now if she wanted to instead of working for wages. Her old man's worth fifty millions if he's worth a cent."

"Then what's she working on a paper for?—keeping some poor devil out of a job."

"She and the old man fell out, had a tiff or something, about the time he started to clean up San Francisco. She quit. That's all—left home and got a job. And let me tell you one thing, Pat: she can everlastingly sling English. There isn't a pen-pusher on the Coast can touch her when she gets going."

36

Pat began to show interest, and Stubener hurried on.

"She writes poetry, too—the regular la-de-dah stuff, just like you. Only I guess hers is better, because she published a whole book of it once. And she writes up the shows. She interviews every big actor that hits this burg."

"I've seen her name in the papers," Pat commented.

"Sure you have. And you're honored, Pat, by her coming to interview you. It won't bother you any. I'll stick right by and give her most of the dope myself. You know I've always done that."

Pat looked his gratitude.

"And another thing, Pat: don't forget you've got to put up with this interviewing. It's part of your business. It's big advertising, and it comes free. We can't buy it. It interests people, draws the crowds, and it's crowds that pile up the gate receipts." He stopped and listened, then looked at his watch. "I think that's her now. I'll go and get her and bring her in. I'll tip it off to her to cut it short, you know, and it won't take long." He turned in the doorway. "And be decent, Pat. Don't shut up like a clam. Talk a bit to her when she asks you questions."

Pat put the Sonnets on the table, took up a newspaper, and was apparently deep in its contents when the two entered the room and he stood up. The meeting was a mutual shock. When blue eyes met gray, it was almost as if the man and the woman shouted triumphantly to each other, as if each had found something sought and unexpected. But this was for the instant only. Each had anticipated in the other something so totally different that the next moment the clear cry of recognition gave way to confusion. As is the way of women, she was the first to achieve control, and she did

37

it without having given any outward sign that she had ever lost it. She advanced most of the distance across the floor to meet Glendon. As for him, he scarcely knew how he stumbled through the introduction. Here was a woman, a WOMAN. He had not known that such a creature could exist. The few women he had noticed had never prefigured this. He wondered what Old Pat's judgment would have been of her, if she was the sort he had recommended to hang on to with both his hands. He discovered that in some way he was holding her hand. He looked at it, curious and fascinated, marveling at its fragility.

She, on the other hand, had proceeded to obliterate the echoes of that first clear call. It had been a peculiar experience, that was all, this sudden out-rush of her toward this strange man. For was not he the abysmal brute of the prize-ring, the great, fighting, stupid bulk of a male animal who hammered up his fellow males of the same stupid order? She smiled at the way he continued to hold her hand.

"I'll have it back, please, Mr. Glendon," she said. "I ... I really need it, you know."

He looked at her blankly, followed her gaze to her imprisoned hand, and dropped it in a rush of awkwardness that sent the blood in a manifest blush to his face.

She noted the blush, and the thought came to her that he did not seem quite the uncouth brute she had pictured. She could not conceive of a brute blushing at anything. And also, she found herself pleased with the fact that he lacked the easy glibness to murmur an apology. But the way he devoured her with his eyes was disconcerting. He stared at her as if in a trance, while his cheeks flushed even more redly.

38

Stubener by this time had fetched a chair for her, and Glendon automatically sank down into his.

"He's in fine shape, Miss Sangster, in fine shape," the manager was saying. "That's right, isn't it, Pat? Never felt better in your life?"

Glendon was bothered by this. His brows contracted in a troubled way, and he made no reply.

"I've wanted to meet you for a long time, Mr. Glendon," Miss Sangster said. "I never interviewed a pugilist before, so if I don't go about it expertly you'll forgive me, I am sure."

"Maybe you'd better start in by seeing him in action," was the manager's suggestion. "While he's getting into his fighting togs I can tell you a lot about him—fresh stuff, too. We'll call in Walsh, Pat, and go a couple of rounds."

"We'll do nothing of the sort," Glendon growled roughly, in just the way an abysmal brute should. "Go ahead with the interview."

The business went ahead unsatisfactorily. Stubener did most of the talking and suggesting, which was sufficient to irritate Maud Sangster, while Pat volunteered nothing. She studied his fine countenance, the eyes clear blue and wide apart, the well-modeled, almost aquiline, nose, the firm, chaste lips that were sweet in a masculine way in their curl at the corners and that gave no hint of any sullenness. It was a baffling personality, she concluded, if what the papers said of him was so. In vain she sought for earmarks of the brute. And in vain she attempted to establish contacts. For one thing, she knew too little about prize-fighters and the ring, and whenever she opened up a lead it was promptly snatched away by the information-oozing Stubener.

"It must be most interesting, this life of a pugilist," she said once, adding with a sigh, "I wish I knew more about it. Tell me: why do you fight?—Oh, aside from money reasons." (This latter to forestall Stubener). "Do you enjoy fighting? Are you stirred by it, by pitting yourself against other men? I hardly know how to express what I mean, so you must be patient with me."

Pat and Stubener began speaking together, but for once Pat bore his manager down.

"I didn't care for it at first—"

"You see, it was too dead easy for him," Stubener interrupted.

"But later," Pat went on, "when I encountered the better fighters, the real big clever ones, where I was more—"

"On your mettle?" she suggested.

"Yes; that's it, more on my mettle, I found I did care for it … a great deal, in fact. But still, it's not so absorbing to me as it might be. You see, while each battle is a sort of problem which I must work out with my wits and muscle, yet to me the issue is never in doubt—"

"He's never had a fight go to a decision," Stubener proclaimed. "He's won every battle by the knock-out route."

"And it's this certainty of the outcome that robs it of what I imagine must be its finest thrills," Pat concluded.

"Maybe you'll get some of them thrills when you go up against Jim Hanford," said the manager.

Pat smiled, but did not speak.

"Tell me some more," she urged, "more about the way you feel when you are fighting."

40

And then Pat amazed his manager, Miss Sangster, and himself, by blurting out:

"It seems to me I don't want to talk with you on such things. It's as if there are things more important for you and me to talk about. I"

He stopped abruptly, aware of what he was saying but unaware of why he was saying it.

"Yes," she cried eagerly. "That's it. That is what makes a good interview — the real personality, you know."

But Pat remained tongue-tied, and Stubener wandered away on a statistical comparison of his champion's weights, measurements, and expansions with those of Sandow, the Terrible Turk, Jeffries, and the other modern strong men. This was of little interest to Maud Sangster, and she showed that she was bored. Her eyes chanced to rest on the Sonnets. She picked the book up and glanced inquiringly at Stubener.

"That's Pat's," he said. "He goes in for that kind of stuff, and color photography, and art exhibits, and such things. But for heaven's sake don't publish anything about it. It would ruin his reputation."

She looked accusingly at Glendon, who immediately became awkward. To her it was delicious. A shy young man, with the body of a giant, who was one of the kings of bruisers, and who read poetry, and went to art exhibits, and experimented with color photography! Of a surety there was no abysmal brute here. His very shyness she divined now was due to sensitiveness and not stupidity. Shakespeare's Sonnets! This was a phase that would bear investigation. But Stubener stole the opportunity away and was back chanting his everlasting statistics.

A few minutes later, and most unwittingly, she opened up the biggest lead of all. That first sharp attraction toward him had begun to stir again after the discovery of the Sonnets. The magnificent frame of his, the handsome face, the chaste lips, the clear-looking eyes, the fine forehead which the short crop of blond hair did not hide, the aura of physical well-being and cleanness which he seemed to emanate—all this, and more that she sensed, drew her as she had never been drawn by any man, and yet through her mind kept running the nasty rumors that she had heard only the day before at the "Courier-Journal" office.

"You were right," she said. "There is something more important to talk about. There is something in my mind I want you to reconcile for me. Do you mind?"

Pat shook his head.

"If I am frank?—abominably frank? I've heard the men, sometimes, talking of particular fights and of the betting odds, and, while I gave no heed to it at the time, it seemed to me it was firmly agreed that there was a great deal of trickery and cheating connected with the sport. Now, when I look at you, for instance, I find it hard to understand how you can be a party to such cheating. I can understand your liking the sport for a sport, as well as for the money it brings you, but I can't understand—"

"There's nothing to understand," Stubener broke in, while Pat's lips were wreathed in a gentle, tolerant smile. "It's all fairy tales, this talk about faking, about fixed fights, and all that rot. There's nothing to it, Miss Sangster, I assure you. And now let me tell you about how I discovered Mr. Glendon. It was a letter I got from his father—"

42

But Maud Sangster refused to be side-tracked, and addressed herself to Pat.

"Listen. I remember one case particularly. It was some fight that took place several months ago—I forget the contestants. One of the editors of the "Courier-Journal" told me he intended to make a good winning. He didn't hope; he said he intended. He said he was on the inside and was betting on the number of rounds. He told me the fight would end in the nineteenth. This was the night before. And the next day he triumphantly called my attention to the fact that it had ended in that very round. I didn't think anything of it one way or the other. I was not interested in prize-fighting then. But I am now. At the time it seemed quite in accord with the vague conception I had about fighting. So you see, it isn't all fairy tales, is it?"

"I know that fight," Glendon said. "It was Owen and Murgweather. And it did end in the nineteenth round, Sam. And she said she heard that round named the day before. How do you account for it, Sam?"

"How do you account for a man picking a lucky lottery ticket?" the manager evaded, while getting his wits together to answer. "That's the very point. Men who study form and condition and seconds and rules and such things often pick the number of rounds, just as men have been known to pick hundred-to-one shots in the races. And don't forget one thing: for every man that wins, there's another that loses, there's another that didn't pick right. Miss Sangster, I assure you, on my honor, that faking and fixing in the fight game is … is non-existent."

"What is your opinion, Mr. Glendon?" she asked.

"The same as mine," Stubener snatched the answer. "He knows

43

what I say is true, every word of it. He's never fought anything but a straight fight in his life. Isn't that right, Pat?"

"Yes; it's right," Pat affirmed, and the peculiar thing to Maud Sangster was that she was convinced he spoke the truth.

She brushed her forehead with her hand, as if to rid herself of the bepuzzlement that clouded her brain.

"Listen," she said. "Last night the same editor told me that your forthcoming fight was arranged to the very round in which it would end."

Stubener was verging on a panic, but Pat's speech saved him from replying.

"Then the editor lies," Pat's voice boomed now for the first time.

"He did not lie before, about that other fight," she challenged.

"What round did he say my fight with Nat Powers would end in?"

Before she could answer, the manager was into the thick of it.

"Oh, rats, Pat!" he cried. "Shut up. It's only the regular run of ring rumors. Let's get on with this interview."

He was ignored by Glendon, whose eyes, bent on hers, were no longer mildly blue, but harsh and imperative. She was sure now that she had stumbled on something tremendous, something that would explain all that had baffled her. At the same time she thrilled to the mastery of his voice and gaze. Here was a male man who would take hold of life and shake out of it what he wanted.

"What round did the editor say?" Glendon reiterated his demand.

"For the love of Mike, Pat, stop this foolishness," Stubener broke in.

"I wish you would give me a chance to answer," Maud Sangster said.

"I guess I'm able to talk with Miss Sangster," Glendon added. "You get out, Sam. Go off and take care of that photographer."

They looked at each other for a tense, silent moment, then the manager moved slowly to the door, opened it, and turned his head to listen.

"And now what round did he say?"

"I hope I haven't made a mistake," she said tremulously, "but I am very sure that he said the sixteenth round."

She saw surprise and anger leap into Glendon's face, and the anger and accusation in the glance he cast at his manager, and she knew the blow had driven home.

And there was reason for his anger. He knew he had talked it over with Stubener, and they had reached a decision to give the audience a good run for its money without unnecessarily prolonging the fight, and to end it in the sixteenth. And here was a woman, from a newspaper office, naming the very round.

Stubener, in the doorway, looked limp and pale, and it was evident he was holding himself together by an effort.

"I'll see you later," Pat told him. "Shut the door behind you."

The door closed, and the two were left alone. Glendon did not speak. The expression on his face was frankly one of trouble and perplexity.

"Well?" she asked.

45

He got up and towered above her, then sat down again, moistening his lips with his tongue.

"I'll tell you one thing," he finally said "The fight won't end in the sixteenth round."

She did not speak, but her unconvinced and quizzical smile hurt him.

"You wait and see, Miss Sangster, and you'll see that editor man is mistaken."

"You mean the program is to be changed?" she queried audaciously.

He quivered to the cut of her words.

"I am not accustomed to lying," he said stiffly, "even to women."

"Neither have you to me, nor have you denied the program is to be changed. Perhaps, Mr. Glendon, I am stupid, but I fail to see the difference in what number the final round occurs so long as it is predetermined and known."

"I'll tell you that round, and not another soul shall know."

She shrugged her shoulders and smiled.

"It sounds to me very much like a racing tip. They are always given that way, you know. Furthermore, I am not quite stupid, and I know there is something wrong here. Why were you made angry by my naming the round? Why were you angry with your manager? Why did you send him from the room?"

For reply, Glendon walked over to the window, as if to look out, where he changed his mind and partly turned, and she knew, without seeing, that he was studying her face. He came back and sat down.

"You've said I haven't lied to you, Miss Sangster, and you were right. I haven't." He paused, groping painfully for a correct statement of the situation. "Now do you think you can believe what I am going to tell you? Will you take the word of a … prize-fighter?"

She nodded gravely, looking him straight in the eyes and certain that what he was about to tell was the truth.

"I've always fought straight and square. I've never touched a piece of dirty money in my life, nor attempted a dirty trick. Now I can go on from that. You've shaken me up pretty badly by what you told me. I don't know what to make of it. I can't pass a snap judgment on it. I don't know. But it looks bad. That's what troubles me. For see you, Stubener and I have talked this fight over, and it was understood between us that I would end the fight in the sixteenth round. Now you bring the same word. How did that editor know? Not from me. Stubener must have let it out … unless…." He stopped to debate the problem. "Unless that editor is a lucky guesser. I can't make up my mind about it. I'll have to keep my eyes open and wait and learn. Every word I've given you is straight, and there's my hand on it."

Again he towered out of his chair and over to her. Her small hand was gripped in his big one as she arose to meet him, and after a fair, straight look into the eyes between them, both glanced unconsciously at the clasped hands. She felt that she had never been more aware that she was a woman. The sex emphasis of those two hands—the soft and fragile feminine and the heavy, muscular masculine—was startling. Glendon was the first to speak.

"You could be hurt so easily," he said; and at the same time she felt the firmness of his grip almost caressingly relax.

She remembered the old Prussian king's love for giants, and laughed at the incongruity of the thought-association as she withdrew her hand.

"I am glad you came here to-day," he said, then hurried on awkwardly to make an explanation which the warm light of admiration in his eyes belied. "I mean because maybe you have opened my eyes to the crooked dealing that has been going on."

"You have surprised me," she urged. "It seemed to me that it is so generally understood that prize-fighting is full of crookedness, that I cannot understand how you, one of its chief exponents, could be ignorant of it. I thought as a matter of course that you would know all about it, and now you have convinced me that you never dreamed of it. You must be different from other fighters."

He nodded his head.

"That explains it, I guess. And that's what comes of keeping away from it—from the other fighters, and promoters, and sports. It was easy to pull the wool over my eyes. Yet it remains to be seen whether it has really been pulled over or not. You see, I am going to find out for myself."

"And change it?" she queried, rather breathlessly, convinced somehow that he could do anything he set out to accomplish.

"No; quit it," was his answer. "If it isn't straight I won't have anything more to do with it. And one thing is certain: this coming fight with Nat Powers won't end in the sixteenth round. If there is any truth in that editor's tip, they'll all be fooled. Instead of putting him out in the sixteenth, I'll let the fight run on into the twenties. You wait and see."

"And I'm not to tell the editor?"

She was on her feet now, preparing to go.

"Certainly not. If he is only guessing, let him take his chances. And if there's anything rotten about it he deserves to lose all he bets. This is to be a little secret between you and me. I'll tell you what I'll do. I'll name the round to you. I won't run it into the twenties. I'll stop Nat Powers in the eighteenth."

"And I'll not whisper it," she assured him.

"I'd like to ask you a favor," he said tentatively. "Maybe it's a big favor."

She showed her acquiescence in her face, as if it were already granted, and he went on:

"Of course, I know you won't use this faking in the interview. But I want more than that. I don't want you to publish anything at all."

She gave him a quick look with her searching gray eyes, then surprised herself by her answer.

"Certainly," she said. "It will not be published. I won't write a line of it."

"I knew it," he said simply.

For the moment she was disappointed by the lack of thanks, and the next moment she was glad that he had not thanked her. She sensed the different foundation he was building under this meeting of an hour with her, and she became daringly explorative.

49

"How did you know it?" she asked.

"I don't know." He shook his head. "I can't explain it. I knew it as a matter of course. Somehow it seems to me I know a lot about you and me."

"But why not publish the interview? As your manager says, it is good advertising."

"I know it," he answered slowly. "But I don't want to know you that way. I think it would hurt if you should publish it. I don't want to think that I knew you professionally. I'd like to remember our talk here as a talk between a man and a woman. I don't know whether you understand what I'm driving at. But it's the way I feel. I want to remember this just as a man and a woman."

As he spoke, in his eyes was all the expression with which a man looks at a woman. She felt the force and beat of him, and she felt strangely tongue-tied and awkward before this man who had been reputed tongue-tied and awkward. He could certainly talk straighter to the point and more convincingly than most men, and what struck her most forcibly was her own inborn certainty that it was mere naïve and simple frankness on his part and not a practised artfulness.

He saw her into her machine, and gave her another thrill when he said good-by. Once again their hands were clasped as he said:

"Some day I'll see you again. I want to see you again. Somehow I have a feeling that the last word has not been said between us."

And as the machine rolled away she was aware of a similar feeling. She had not seen the last of this very disquieting Pat Glendon, king of the bruisers and abysmal brute.

50

Back in the training quarters, Glendon encountered his perturbed manager.

"What did you fire me out for?" Stubener demanded. "We're finished. A hell of a mess you've made. You've never stood for meeting a reporter alone before, and now you'll see when that interview comes out."

Glendon, who had been regarding him with cool amusement, made as if to turn and pass on, and then changed his mind.

"It won't come out," he said.

Stubener looked up sharply.

"I asked her not to," Glendon explained.

Then Stubener exploded.

"As if she'd kill a juicy thing like that."

Glendon became very cold and his voice was harsh and grating.

"It won't be published. She told me so. And to doubt it is to call her a liar."

The Irish flame was in his eyes, and by that, and by the unconscious clenching of his passion-wrought hands, Stubener, who knew the strength of them, and of the man he faced, no longer dared to doubt.

VII

It did not take Stubener long to find out that Glendon intended extending the distance of the fight, though try as he would he could get no hint of the number of the round. He wasted no time, however, and privily clinched certain arrangements with Nat Powers and Nat Powers' manager. Powers had a faithful following of bettors, and the betting syndicate was not to be denied its harvest.

On the night of the fight, Maud Sangster was guilty of a more daring unconventionality than any she had yet committed, though no whisper of it leaked out to shock society. Under the protection of the editor, she occupied a ring-side seat. Her hair and most of her face were hidden under a slouch hat, while she wore a man's long overcoat that fell to her heels. Entering in the thick of the crowd, she was not noticed; nor did the newspaper men, in the press seats against the ring directly in front of her, recognize her.

As was the growing custom, there were no preliminary bouts, and she had barely gained her seat when roars of applause announced the arrival of Nat Powers. He came down the aisle in the midst of his seconds, and she was almost frightened by the formidable bulk of him. Yet he leaped the ropes as lightly as a man half his weight, and grinned acknowledgment to the tumultuous greeting that arose from all the house. He was not pretty. Two cauliflower ears attested his profession and its attendant brutality, while his broken nose had been so often spread over his face as to defy the surgeon's art to reconstruct it.

Another uproar heralded the arrival of Glendon, and she watched him eagerly as he went through the ropes to his corner. But it was not until the tedious time of announcements, introductions, and challenges was over, that the two men threw off their wraps and faced each other in ring costume. Concentrated upon them from overhead was the white glare of many electric lights—this for the benefit of the moving picture cameras; and she felt, as she looked at the two sharply contrasted men, that it was in Glendon that she saw the thoroughbred and in Powers the abysmal brute. Both looked their parts—Glendon, clean cut in face and form, softly and massively beautiful, Powers almost asymmetrically rugged and heavily matted with hair.

As they made their preliminary pose 1for the cameras, confronting each other in fighting attitudes, it chanced that Glendon's gaze dropped down through the ropes and rested on her face. Though he gave no sign, she knew, with a swift leap of the heart, that he had recognized her. The next moment the gong sounded, the announcer cried "Let her go!" and the battle was on.

It was a good fight. There was no blood, no marring, and both were clever. Half of the first round was spent in feeling each other out, but Maud Sangster found the play and feint and tap of the gloves sufficiently exciting. During some of the fiercer rallies in later stages of the fight, the editor was compelled to touch her arm to remind her who she was and where she was.

Powers fought easily and cleanly, as became the hero of half a hundred ring battles, and an admiring claque applauded 1his every cleverness. Yet he did not unduly exert himself save in occasional strenuous rallies that brought the audience yelling to its feet in the mistaken notion that he was getting his man.

It was at such a moment, when her unpractised eye could not inform her that Glendon was escaping serious damage, that the editor leaned to her and said:

"Young Pat will win all right. He's a comer, and they can't stop him. But he'll win in the sixteenth and not before."

"Or after?" she asked.

She almost laughed at the certitude of her companion's negative. She knew better.

Powers was noted for hunting his man from moment to moment and round to round, and Glendon was content to accede to this program. His defense was admirable, and he threw in just enough of offense to whet the edge of the 1audience's interest. Though he knew he was scheduled to lose, Powers had had too long a ring experience to hesitate from knocking his man out if the opportunity offered. He had had the double cross worked too often on him to be chary in working it on others. If he got his chance he was prepared to knock his man out and let the syndicate go hang. Thanks to clever press publicity, the idea was prevalent that at last Young Glendon had met his master. In his heart, Powers, however, knew that it was himself who had encountered the better man. More than once, in the faster in-fighting, he received the weight of punches that he knew had been deliberately made no heavier.

On Glendon's part, there were times and times when a slip or error of judgment could have exposed him to one of his antagonist's sledge-hammer blows and 1lost him the fight. Yet his was that almost miraculous power of accurate timing and distancing, and his confidence was not shaken by the several close shaves he experienced. He had never lost a fight, never been knocked down, and he had always been so thoroughly the master of the man he faced, that such a possibility was unthinkable.

At the end of the fifteenth round, both men were in good condition,

54

though Powers was breathing a trifle heavily and there were men in the ringside seats offering odds that he would "blow up."

It was just before the gong for the sixteenth round struck that Stubener, leaning over Glendon from behind in his corner, whispered:

"Are you going to get him now?"

Glendon, with a back toss of his head, shook it and laughed mockingly up into his manager's anxious face. 1

With the stroke of the gong for the sixteenth round, Glendon was surprised to see Powers cut loose. From the first second it was a tornado of fighting, and Glendon was hard put to escape serious damage. He blocked, clinched, ducked, sidestepped, was rushed backward against the ropes and was met by fresh rushes when he surged out to center. Several times Powers left inviting openings, but Glendon refused to loose the lightning-bolt of a blow that would drop his man. He was reserving that blow for two rounds later. Not in the whole fight had he ever exerted his full strength, nor struck with the force that was in him.

For two minutes, without the slightest let-up, Powers went at him hammer and tongs. In another minute the round would be over and the betting syndicate hard hit. But that minute was not to be. They had just come together in the 1center of the ring. It was as ordinary a clinch as any in the fight, save that Powers was struggling and roughing it every instant. Glendon whipped his left over in a crisp but easy jolt to the side of the face. It was like any of a score of similar jolts he had already delivered in the course of the fight. To his amazement he felt Powers go limp in his arms and begin sinking to the floor on sagging, spraddling legs that refused to bear his weight. He struck the floor with a thump, rolled half over on his side, and lay with closed eyes and motionless. The referee, bending above him, was shouting the count.

At the cry of "Nine!" Powers quivered as if making a vain effort to rise.

"Ten!—and out!" cried the referee.

He caught Glendon's hand and raised it aloft to the roaring audience in token that he was the winner. 1

For the first time in the ring, Glendon was dazed. It had not been a knockout blow. He could stake his life on that. It had not been to the jaw but to the side of the face, and he knew it had gone there and nowhere else. Yet the man was out, had been counted out, and he had faked it beautifully. That final thump on the floor had been a convincing masterpiece. To the audience it was indubitably a knockout, and the moving picture machines would perpetuate the lie. The editor had called the turn after all, and a crooked turn it was.

Glendon shot a swift glance through the ropes to the face of Maud Sangster. She was looking straight at him, but her eyes were bleak and hard, and there was neither recognition nor expression in them. Even as he looked, she turned away unconcernedly and said something to the man beside her. 1

Powers' seconds were carrying him to his corner, a seeming limp wreck of a man. Glendon's seconds were advancing upon him to congratulate him and to remove his gloves. But Stubener was ahead of them. His face was beaming as he caught Glendon's right glove in both his hands and cried:

56

"Good boy, Pat. I knew you'd do it."

Glendon pulled his glove away. And for the first time in the years they had been together, his manager heard him swear.

"You go to hell," he said, and turned to hold out his hands for his seconds to pull off the gloves. 1

VIII

That night, after receiving the editor's final dictum that there was not a square fighter in the game, Maud Sangster cried quietly for a moment on the edge of her bed, grew angry, and went to sleep hugely disgusted with herself, prize-fighters, and the world in general.

The next afternoon she began work on an interview with Henry Addison that was destined never to be finished. It was in the private room that was accorded her at the "Courier-Journal" office that the thing happened. She had paused in her writing to glance at a headline in the afternoon paper announcing that Glendon was matched with Tom Cannam, when 1one of the door-boys brought in a card. It was Glendon's.

"Tell him I can't be seen," she told the boy.

In a minute he was back.

"He says he's coming in anyway, but he'd rather have your permission."

"Did you tell him I was busy?" she asked.

"Yes'm, but he said he was coming just the same."

She made no answer, and the boy, his eyes shining with admiration for the importunate visitor, rattled on.

"I know'm. He's a awful big guy. If he started roughhousing he could clean the whole office out. He's young Glendon, who won the fight last night."

"Very well, then. Bring him in. We don't want the office cleaned out, you know."

No greetings were exchanged when Glendon entered. She was as cold and inhospitable as a gray day, and neither invited him to a chair nor recognized him with her eyes, sitting half turned away from him at her desk and waiting for him to state his business. He gave no sign of how this cavalier treatment affected him, but plunged directly into his subject.

"I want to talk to you," he said shortly. "That fight. It did end in that round."

She shrugged her shoulders.

"I knew it would."

"You didn't," he retorted. "You didn't. I didn't."

She turned and looked at him with quiet affectation of boredom.

"What is the use?" she asked. "Prize-fighting is prize-fighting, and we all know what it means. The fight did end in the round I told you it would."

"It did," he agreed. "But you didn't know it would. In all the world you and I were at least two that knew Powers wouldn't be knocked out in the sixteenth."

She remained silent.

"I say you knew he wouldn't." He spoke peremptorily, and, when she still declined to speak, stepped nearer to her. "Answer me," he commanded.

She nodded her head.

"But he was," she insisted.

"He wasn't. He wasn't knocked out at all. Do you get that? I am going to tell you about it, and you are going to listen. I didn't lie to you. Do you get that? I didn't lie to you. I was a fool, and they fooled me, and you along with me. You thought you saw him knocked out. Yet the blow I struck was not heavy enough. It didn't hit him in the right place either. He made believe it did. He faked that knockout."

He paused and looked at her expectantly. And somehow, with a leap and thrill, she knew that she believed him, and she felt pervaded by a warm happiness at the reinstatement of this man who meant nothing to her and whom she had seen but twice in her life.

"Well?" he demanded, and she thrilled anew at the compellingness of him.

59

She stood up, and her hand went out to his.

"I believe you," she said. "And I am glad, most glad."

It was a longer grip than she had anticipated. He looked at her with eyes that burned and to which her own unconsciously answered back. Never was there such a man, was her thought. Her eyes dropped first, and his followed, so that, as before, both gazed at the clasped hands. He made a movement of his whole body toward her, impulsive and involuntary, as if to gather her to him, then checked himself abruptly, with an unmistakable effort. She saw it, and felt the pull of his hand as it started to draw her to him. And to her amazement she felt the desire to yield, the desire almost overwhelmingly to be drawn into the strong circle of those arms. And had he compelled, she knew that she would not have refrained. She was almost dizzy, when he checked himself and with a closing of his fingers that half crushed hers, dropped her hand, almost flung it from him.

"God!" he breathed. "You were made for me."

He turned partly away from her, sweeping his hand to his forehead. She knew she would hate him forever if he dared one stammered word of apology or explanation. But he seemed to have the way always of doing the right thing where she was concerned. She sank into her chair, and he into another, first drawing it around so as to face her across the corner of the desk.

"I spent last night in a Turkish bath," he said. "I sent for an old broken-down bruiser. He was a friend of my father in the old days. I knew there couldn't be a thing about the ring he didn't know, and I made him talk. The funny thing was that it was all I could do to convince him that I didn't know the things I asked him about. He

60

called me the babe in the woods. I guess he was right. I was raised in the woods, and woods is about all I know.

"Well, I received an education from that old man last night. The ring is rottener than you told me. It seems everybody connected with it is crooked. The very supervisors that grant the fight permits graft off of the promoters; and the promoters, managers, and fighters graft off of each other and off the public. It's down to a system, in one way, and on the other hand they're always—do you know what the double cross is?" (She nodded.) "Well, they don't seem to miss a chance to give each other the double cross.

"The stuff that old man told me took my breath away. And here I've been in the thick of it for several years and knew nothing of it. I was a real babe in the woods. And yet I can see how I've been fooled. I was so made that nobody could stop me. I was bound to win, and, thanks to Stubener, everything crooked was kept away from me. This morning I cornered Spider Walsh and made him talk. He was my first trainer, you know, and he followed Stubener's instructions. They kept me in ignorance. Besides, I didn't herd with the sporting crowd. I spent my time hunting and fishing and monkeying with cameras and such things. Do you know what Walsh and Stubener called me between themselves?—the Virgin. I only learned it this morning from Walsh, and it was like pulling teeth. And they were right. I was a little innocent lamb.

"And Stubener was using me for crookedness, too, only I didn't know it. I can look back now and see how it was worked. But you see, I wasn't interested enough in the game to be suspicious. I was born with a good body and a cool head, I was raised in the open, and I was taught by my father, who knew more about fighting than any man living or dead. It was too easy. The ring didn't absorb me.

61

There was never any doubt of the outcome. But I'm done with it now."

She pointed to the headline announcing his match with Tom Cannam.

"That's Stubener's work," he explained. "It was programmed months ago. But I don't care. I'm heading for the mountains. I've quit."

She glanced at the unfinished interview on the desk and sighed.

"How lordly men are," she said. "Masters of destiny. They do as they please—"

"From what I've heard," he interrupted, "you've done pretty much as you please. It's one of the things I like about you. And what has struck me hard from the first was the way you and I understand each other."

He broke off and looked at her with burning eyes.

"Well, the ring did one thing for me," he went on. "It made me acquainted with you. And when you find the one woman, there's just one thing to do. Take her in your two hands and don't let go. Come on, let us start for the mountains."

It had come with the suddenness of a thunder-clap, and yet she felt that she had been expecting it. Her heart was beating up and almost choking her in a strangely delicious way. Here at least was the primitive and the simple with a vengeance. Then, too, it seemed a dream. Such things did not take place in modern newspaper offices. Love could not be made in such fashion; it only so occurred on the stage and in novels.

He had arisen, and was holding out both hands to her.

62

"I don't dare," she said in a whisper, half to herself. "I don't dare."

And thereat she was stung by the quick contempt that flashed in his eyes but that swiftly changed to open incredulity.

"You'd dare anything you wanted," he was saying. "I know that. It's not a case of dare, but of want. Do you want?"

She had arisen, and was now swaying as if in a dream. It flashed into her mind to wonder if it were hypnotism. She wanted to glance about her at the familiar objects of the room in order to identify herself with reality, but she could not take her eyes from his. Nor did she speak.

He had stepped beside her. His hand was on her arm, and she leaned toward him involuntarily. It was all part of the dream, and it was no longer hers to question anything. It was the great dare. He was right. She could dare what she wanted, and she did want. He was helping her into her jacket. She was thrusting the hat-pins through her hair. And even as she realized it, she found herself walking beside him through the opened door. The "Flight of the Duchess" and "The Statue and the Bust," darted through her mind. Then she remembered "Waring."

"'What's become of Waring?'" she murmured.

"'Land travel or sea-faring?'" he murmured back.

And to her this kindred sufficient note was a vindication of her madness.

At the entrance of the building he raised his hand to call a taxi, but was stopped by her touch on his arm.

"Where are we going?" she breathed.

"To the Ferry. We've just time to catch that Sacramento train."

"But I can't go this way," she protested. "I ... I haven't even a change of handkerchiefs."

He held up his hand again before replying.

"You can shop in Sacramento. We'll get married there and catch the night overland north. I'll arrange everything by telegraph from the train."

As the cab drew to the curb, she looked quickly about her at the familiar street and the familiar throng, then, with almost a flurry of alarm, into Glendon's face.

"I don't know a thing about you," she said.

"We know everything about each other," was his answer.

She felt the support and urge of his arms, and lifted her foot to the step. The next moment the door had closed, he was beside her, and the cab was heading down Market Street. He passed his arm around her, drew her close, and kissed her. When next she glimpsed his face she was certain that it was dyed with a faint blush.

"I ... I've heard there was an art in kissing," he stammered. "I don't know anything about it myself, but I'll learn. You see, you're the first woman I ever kissed."

IX

Where a jagged peak of rock thrust above the vast virgin forest, reclined a man and a woman. Beneath them, on the edge of the trees, were tethered two horses. Behind each saddle were a pair of small saddle-bags. The trees were monotonously huge. Towering hundreds of feet into the air, they ran from eight to ten and twelve feet in diameter. Many were much larger. All morning they had toiled up the divide through this unbroken forest, and this peak of rock had been the first spot where they could get out of the forest in order to see the forest.

Beneath them and away, far as they could see, lay range upon range of haze-empurpled mountains. There was no end to these ranges. They rose one behind another to the dim, distant skyline, where they faded away with a vague promise of unending extension beyond. There were no clearings in the forest; north, south, east, and west, untouched, unbroken, it covered the land with its mighty growth.

They lay, feasting their eyes on the sight, her hand clasped in one of his; for this was their honeymoon, and these were the redwoods of Mendocino. Across from Shasta they had come, with horses and saddle-bags, and down through the wilds of the coast counties, and they had no plan except to continue until some other plan entered their heads. They were roughly dressed, she in travel-stained khaki, he in overalls and woolen shirt. The latter was open at the sunburned neck, and in his hugeness he seemed a fit dweller among the forest giants, while for her, as a dweller with him, there were no signs of aught else but happiness.

65

"Well, Big Man," she said, propping herself up on an elbow to gaze at him, "it is more wonderful than you promised. And we are going through it together."

"And there's a lot of the rest of the world we'll go through together," he answered, shifting his position so as to get her hand in both of his.

"But not till we've finished with this," she urged. "I seem never to grow tired of the big woods ... and of you."

He slid effortlessly into a sitting posture and gathered her into his arms.

"Oh, you lover," she whispered. "And I had given up hope of finding such a one."

"And I never hoped at all. I must just have known all the time that I was going to find you. Glad?"

Her answer was a soft pressure where her hand rested on his neck, and for long minutes they looked out over the great woods and dreamed.

"You remember I told you how I ran away from the red-haired school teacher? That was the first time I saw this country. I was on foot, but forty or fifty miles a day was play for me. I was a regular Indian. I wasn't thinking about you then. Game was pretty scarce in the redwoods, but there was plenty of fine trout. That was when I camped on these rocks. I didn't dream that some day I'd be back with you, YOU."

"And be a champion of the ring, too," she suggested.

"No; I didn't think about that at all. Dad had always told me I was going to be, and I took it for granted. You see, he was very wise. He was a great man."

"But he didn't see you leaving the ring."

"I don't know. He was so careful in hiding its crookedness from me, that I think he feared it. I've told you about the contract with Stubener. Dad put in that clause about crookedness. The first crooked thing my manager did was to break the contract."

"And yet you are going to fight this Tom Cannam. Is it worth while?"

He looked at her quickly.

"Don't you want me to?"

"Dear lover, I want you to do whatever you want."

So she said, and to herself, her words still ringing in her ears, she marveled that she, not least among the stubbornly independent of the breed of Sangster, should utter them. Yet she knew they were true, and she was glad.

"It will be fun," he said.

"But I don't understand all the gleeful details."

"I haven't worked them out yet. You might help me. In the first place I'm going to double-cross Stubener and the betting syndicate. It will be part of the joke. I am going to put Cannam out in the first round. For the first time I shall be really angry when I fight. Poor Tom Cannam, who's as crooked as the rest, will be the chief sacrifice. You see, I intend to make a speech in the ring. It's unusual, but it will be a success, for I am going to tell the audience

67

all the inside workings of the game. It's a good game, too, but they're running it on business principles, and that's what spoils it. But there, I'm giving the speech to you instead of at the ring."

"I wish I could be there to hear," she said.

He looked at her and debated.

"I'd like to have you. But it's sure to be a rough time. There is no telling what may happen when I start my program. But I'll come straight to you as soon as it's over. And it will be the last appearance of Young Glendon in the ring, in any ring."

"But, dear, you've never made a speech in your life," she objected. "You might fail."

He shook his head positively.

"I'm Irish," he announced, "and what Irishman was there who couldn't speak?" He paused to laugh merrily. "Stubener thinks I'm crazy. Says a man can't train on matrimony. A lot he knows about matrimony, or me, or you, or anything except real estate and fixed fights. But I'll show him that night, and poor Tom, too. I really feel sorry for Tom."

"My dear abysmal brute is going to behave most abysmally and brutally, I fear," she murmured.

He laughed.

"I'm going to make a noble attempt at it. Positively my last appearance, you know. And then it will be you, YOU. But if you don't want that last appearance, say the word."

"Of course I want it, Big Man. I want my Big Man for himself, and to be himself he must be himself. If you want this, I want it for you, and for myself, too. Suppose I said I wanted to go on the stage, or to the South Seas or the North Pole?"

He answered slowly, almost solemnly.

"Then I'd say go ahead. Because you are you and must be yourself and do whatever you want. I love you because you are you."

"And we're both a silly pair of lovers," she said, when his embrace had relaxed.

"Isn't it great!" he cried.

He stood up, measured the sun with his eye, and extended his hand out over the big woods that covered the serried, purple ranges.

"We've got to sleep out there somewhere. It's thirty miles to the nearest camp."

X

Who, of all the sports present, will ever forget the memorable night at the Golden Gate Arena, when Young Glendon put Tom Cannam to sleep and an even greater one than Tom Cannam, kept the great audience on the ragged edge of riot for an hour, caused the

69

subsequent graft investigation of the supervisors and the indictments of the contractors and the building commissioners, and pretty generally disrupted the whole fight game. It was a complete surprise. Not even Stubener had the slightest apprehension of what was coming. It was true that his man had been insubordinate after the Nat Powers affair, and had run off and got married; but all that was over. Young Pat had done the expected, swallowed the inevitable crookedness of the ring, and come back into it again.

The Golden Gate Arena was new. This was its first fight, and it was the biggest building of the kind San Francisco had ever erected. It seated twenty-five thousand, and every seat was occupied. Sports had traveled from all the world to be present, and they had paid fifty dollars for their ring-side seats. The cheapest seat in the house had sold for five dollars.

The old familiar roar of applause went up when Billy Morgan, the veteran announcer, climbed through the ropes and bared his gray head. As he opened his mouth to speak, a heavy crash came from a near section where several tiers of low seats had collapsed. The crowd broke into loud laughter and shouted jocular regrets and advice to the victims, none of whom had been hurt. The crash of the seats and the hilarious uproar caused the captain of police in charge to look at one of his lieutenants and lift his brows in token that they would have their hands full and a lively night.

One by one, welcomed by uproarious applause, seven doughty old ring heroes climbed through the ropes to be introduced. They were all ex-heavy-weight champions of the world. Billy Morgan accompanied each presentation to the audience with an appropriate phrase. One was hailed as "Honest John" and "Old Reliable," another was "the squarest two-fisted fighter the ring ever saw." And of others: "the hero of a hundred battles and never threw one and never lay down"; "the gamest of the old guard"; "the only one who ever came back"; "the greatest warrior of them all"; and "the hardest nut in the ring to crack."

All this took time. A speech was insisted on from each of them, and they mumbled and muttered in reply with proud blushes and awkward shamblings. The longest speech was from "Old Reliable" and lasted nearly a minute. Then they had to be photographed. The ring filled up with celebrities, with champion wrestlers, famous conditioners, and veteran time-keepers and referees. Light-weights and middle-weights swarmed. Everybody seemed to be challenging everybody. Nat Powers was there, demanding a return match from Young Glendon, and so were all the other shining lights whom Glendon had snuffed out. Also, they all challenged Jim Hanford, who, in turn, had to make his statement, which was to the effect that he would accord the next fight to the winner of the one that was about to take place. The audience immediately proceeded to name the winner, half of it wildly crying "Glendon," and the other half "Powers." In the midst of the pandemonium another tier of seats went down, and half a dozen rows were on between cheated ticket holders and the stewards who had been reaping a fat harvest. The captain despatched a message to headquarters for additional police details.

The crowd was feeling good. When Cannam and Glendon made their ring entrances the Arena resembled a national political convention. Each was cheered for a solid five minutes. The ring was now cleared. Glendon sat in his corner surrounded by his seconds. As usual, Stubener was at his back. Cannam was introduced first, and after he had scraped and ducked his head, he was compelled to respond to the cries for a speech. He stammered and halted, but managed to grind out several ideas.

"I'm proud to be here to-night," he said, and found space to capture another thought while the applause was thundering. "I've fought square. I've fought square all my life. Nobody can deny that. And I'm going to do my best to-night."

There were loud cries of: "That's right, Tom!" "We know that!" "Good boy, Tom!" "You're the boy to fetch the bacon home!"

Then came Glendon's turn. From him, likewise, a speech was demanded, though for principals to give speeches was an unprecedented thing in the prize-ring. Billy Morgan held up his hand for silence, and in a clear, powerful voice Glendon began.

"Everybody has told you they were proud to be here to-night," he said. "I am not" The audience was startled, and he paused long enough to let it sink home, "I am not proud of my company. You wanted a speech. I'll give you a real one. This is my last fight. After to-night I leave the ring for good. Why? I have already told you. I don't like my company. The prize-ring is so crooked that no man engaged in it can hide behind a corkscrew. It is rotten to the core, from the little professional clubs right up to this affair to-night."

The low rumble of astonishment that had been rising at this point burst into a roar. There were loud boos and hisses, and many began crying: "Go on with the fight!" "We want the fight!" "Why don't you fight?" Glendon, waiting, noted that the principal disturbers near the ring were promoters and managers and fighters. In vain did he strive to make himself heard. The audience was divided, half crying out, "Fight!" and the other half, "Speech! Speech!"

Ten minutes of hopeless madness prevailed. Stubener, the referee, the owner of the Arena, and the promoter of the fight, pleaded with Glendon to go on with the fight. When he refused, the referee declared that he would award the fight in forfeit to Cannam if Glendon did not fight.

"You can't do it," the latter retorted. "I'll sue you in all the courts if you try that on, and I'll not promise you that you'll survive this crowd if you cheat it out of the fight. Besides, I'm going to fight. But before I do I'm going to finish my speech."

"But it's against the rules," protested the referee.

"It's nothing of the sort. There's not a word in the rules against ring-side speeches. Every big fighter here to-night has made a speech."

"Only a few words," shouted the promoter in Glendon's ear. "But you're giving a lecture."

"There's nothing in the rules against lectures," Glendon answered. "And now you fellows get out of the ring or I'll throw you out."

The promoter, apoplectic and struggling, was dropped over the ropes by his coat-collar. He was a large man, but so easily had Glendon done it with one hand that the audience went wild with delight. The cries for a speech increased in volume. Stubener and the owner beat a wise retreat. Glendon held up his hands to be heard, whereupon those that shouted for the fight redoubled their efforts. Two or three tiers of seats crashed down, and numbers who had thus lost their places, added to the turmoil by making a concerted rush to squeeze in on the still intact seats, while those behind, blocked from sight of the ring, yelled and raved for them to sit down.

Glendon walked to the ropes and spoke to the police captain. He was compelled to bend over and shout in his ear.

73

"If I don't give this speech," he said, "this crowd will wreck the place. If they break loose you can never hold them, you know that. Now you've got to help. You keep the ring clear and I'll silence the crowd."

He went back to the center of the ring and again held up his hands.

"You want that speech?" he shouted in a tremendous voice.

Hundreds near the ring heard him and cried "Yes!"

"Then let every man who wants to hear shut up the noise-maker next to him!"

The advice was taken, so that when he repeated it, his voice penetrated farther. Again and again he shouted it, and slowly, zone by zone, the silence pressed outward from the ring, accompanied by a muffled undertone of smacks and thuds and scuffles as the obstreperous were subdued by their neighbors. Almost had all confusion been smothered, when a tier of seats near the ring went down. This was greeted with fresh roars of laughter, which of itself died away, so that a lone voice, far back, was heard distinctly as it piped: "Go on, Glendon! We're with you!"

Glendon had the Celt's intuitive knowledge of the psychology of the crowd. He knew that what had been a vast disorderly mob five minutes before was now tightly in hand, and for added effect he deliberately delayed. Yet the delay was just long enough and not a second too long. For thirty seconds the silence was complete, and the effect produced was one of awe. Then, just as the first faint hints of restlessness came to his ears, he began to speak:

"When I finish this speech," he said, "I am going to fight. I promise you it will be a real fight, one of the few real fights you have ever seen. I am going to get my man in the shortest possible time. Billy Morgan, in making his final announcement, will tell you that it is to be a forty-five-round contest. Let me tell you that it will be nearer forty-five seconds.

"When I was interrupted I was telling you that the ring was rotten. It is—from top to bottom. It is run on business principles, and you all know what business principles are. Enough said. You are the suckers, every last one of you that is not making anything out of it. Why are the seats falling down to-night? Graft. Like the fight game, they were built on business principles."

He now held the audience stronger than ever, and knew it.

"There are three men squeezed on two seats. I can see that everywhere. What does it mean? Graft. The stewards don't get any wages. They are supposed to graft. Business principles again. You pay. Of course you pay. How are the fight permits obtained? Graft. And now let me ask you: if the men who build the seats graft, if the stewards graft, if the authorities graft, why shouldn't those higher up in the fight game graft? They do. And you pay.

"And let me tell you it is not the fault of the fighters. They don't run the game. The promoters and managers run it; they're the business men. The fighters are only fighters. They begin honestly enough, but the managers and promoters make them give in or kick them out. There have been straight fighters. And there are now a few, but they don't earn much as a rule. I guess there have been straight managers. Mine is about the best of the boiling. But just ask him how much he's got salted down in real estate and apartment houses."

Here the uproar began to drown his voice.

"Let every man who wants to hear shut up the man alongside of him!" Glendon instructed.

Again, like the murmur of a surf, there was a rustling of smacks, and thuds, and scuffles, and the house quieted down.

"Why does every fighter work overtime insisting that he's always fought square? Why are they called Honest Johns, and Honest Bills, and Honest Blacksmiths, and all the rest? Doesn't it ever strike you that they seem to be afraid of something? When a man comes to you shouting he is honest, you get suspicious. But when a prize-fighter passes the same dope out to you, you swallow it down.

"May the best man win! How often have you heard Billy Morgan say that! Let me tell you that the best man doesn't win so often, and when he does it's usually arranged for him. Most of the grudge fights you've heard or seen were arranged, too. It's a program. The whole thing is programmed. Do you think the promoters and managers are in it for their health? They're not. They're business men.

"Tom, Dick, and Harry are three fighters. Dick is the best man. In two fights he could prove it. But what happens? Tom licks Harry. Dick licks Tom. Harry licks Dick. Nothing proved. Then come the return matches. Harry licks Tom. Tom licks Dick. Dick licks Harry. Nothing proved. Then they try again. Dick is kicking. Says he wants to get along in the game. So Dick licks Tom, and Dick licks Harry. Eight fights to prove Dick the best man, when two could have done it. All arranged. A regular program. And you pay for it, and when your seats don't break down you get robbed of them by the stewards.

"It's a good game, too, if it were only square. The fighters would be

76

square if they had a chance. But the graft is too big. When a handful of men can divide up three-quarters of a million dollars on three fights—"

A wild outburst compelled him to stop. Out of the medley of cries from all over the house, he could distinguish such as "What million dollars?" "What three fights?" "Tell us!" "Go on!" Likewise there were boos and hisses, and cries of "Muckraker! Muckraker!"

"Do you want to hear?" Glendon shouted. "Then keep order!"

Once more he compelled the impressive half minute of silence.

"What is Jim Hanford planning? What is the program his crowd and mine are framing up? They know I've got him. He knows I've got him. I can whip him in one fight. But he's the champion of the world. If I don't give in to the program, they'll never give me a chance to fight him. The program calls for three fights. I am to win the first fight. It will be pulled off in Nevada if San Francisco won't stand for it. We are to make it a good fight. To make it good, each of us will put up a side bet of twenty thousand. It will be real money, but it won't be a real bet. Each gets his own slipped back to him. The same way with the purse. We'll divide it evenly, though the public division will be thirty-five and sixty-five. The purse, the moving picture royalties, the advertisements, and all the rest of the drags won't be a cent less than two hundred and fifty thousand. We'll divide it, and go to work on the return match. Hanford will win that, and we divide again. Then comes the third fight; I win as I have every right to; and we have taken three-quarters of a million out of the pockets of the fighting public. That's the program, but the money is dirty. And that's why I am quitting the ring to-night—"

It was at this moment that Jim Hanford, kicking a clinging

77

policeman back among the seat-holders, heaved his huge frame through the ropes, bellowing:

"It's a lie!"

He rushed like an infuriated bull at Glendon, who sprang back, and then, instead of meeting the rush, ducked cleanly away. Unable to check himself, the big man fetched up against the ropes. Flung back by the spring of them, he was turning to make another rush, when Glendon landed him. Glendon, cool, clear-seeing, distanced his man perfectly to the jaw and struck the first full-strength blow of his career. All his strength, and his reserve of strength, went into that one smashing muscular explosion.

Hanford was dead in the air—in so far as unconsciousness may resemble death. So far as he was concerned, he ceased at the moment of contact with Glendon's fist. His feet left the floor and he was in the air until he struck the topmost rope. His inert body sprawled across it, sagged at the middle, and fell through the ropes and down out of the ring upon the heads of the men in the press seats.

The audience broke loose. It had already seen more than it had paid to see, for the great Jim Hanford, the world champion, had been knocked out. It was unofficial, but it had been with a single punch. Never had there been such a night in fistiana. Glendon looked ruefully at his damaged knuckles, cast a glance through the ropes to where Hanford was groggily coming to, and held up his hands. He had clinched his right to be heard, and the audience grew still.

"When I began to fight," he said, "they called me 'One-Punch Glendon.' You saw that punch a moment ago. I always had that punch. I went after my men and got them on the jump, though I

78

was careful not to hit with all my might. Then I was educated. My manager told me it wasn't fair to the crowd. He advised me to make long fights so that the crowd could get a run for its money. I was a fool, a mutt. I was a green lad from the mountains. So help me God, I swallowed it as the truth. My manager used to talk over with me what round I would put my man out in. Then he tipped it off to the betting syndicate, and the betting syndicate went to it. Of course you paid. But I am glad for one thing. I never touched a cent of the money. They didn't dare offer it to me, because they knew it would give the game away.

"You remember my fight with Nat Powers. I never knocked him out. I had got suspicious. So the gang framed it up with him. I didn't know. I intended to let him go a couple of rounds over the sixteenth. That last punch in the sixteenth didn't shake him. But he faked the knock-out just the same and fooled all of you."

"How about to-night?" a voice called out. "Is it a frame-up?"

"It is," was Glendon's answer. "How's the syndicate betting? That Cannam will last to the fourteenth."

Howls and hoots went up. For the last time Glendon held up his hand for silence.

"I'm almost done now. But I want to tell you one thing. The syndicate gets landed to-night. This is to be a square fight. Tom Cannam won't last till the fourteenth round. He won't last the first round."

Cannam sprang to his feet in his corner and cried out in a fury:

"You can't do it. The man don't live who can get me in one round!"

Glendon ignored him and went on.

79

"Once now in my life I have struck with all my strength. You saw that a moment ago when I caught Hanford. To-night, for the second time, I am going to hit with all my strength—that is, if Cannam doesn't jump through the ropes right now and get away. And now I'm ready."

He went to his corner and held out his hands for his gloves. In the opposite corner Cannam raged while his seconds tried vainly to calm him. At last Billy Morgan managed to make the final announcement.

"This will be a forty-five round contest," he shouted. "Marquis of Queensbury Rules! And may the best man win! Let her go!"

The gong struck. The two men advanced. Glendon's right hand was extended for the customary shake, but Cannam, with an angry toss of the head, refused to take it. To the general surprise, he did not rush. Angry though he was, he fought carefully, his touched pride impelling him to bend every effort to last out the round. Several times he struck, but he struck cautiously, never relaxing his defense. Glendon hunted him about the ring, ever advancing with the remorseless tap-tap of his left foot. Yet he struck no blows, nor attempted to strike. He even dropped his hands to his sides and hunted the other defenselessly in an effort to draw him out. Cannam grinned defiantly, but declined to take advantage of the proffered opening.

Two minutes passed, and then a change came over Glendon. By every muscle, by every line of his face, he advertised that the moment had come for him to get his man. Acting it was, and it was well acted. He seemed to have become a thing of steel, as hard and pitiless as steel. The effect was apparent on Cannam, who redoubled his caution. Glendon quickly worked him into a corner and herded and held him there. Still he struck no blow, nor attempted to strike, and the suspense on Cannam's part grew painful. In vain he tried to work out of the corner, while he could not summon resolution to rush upon his opponent in an attempt to gain the respite of a clinch.

Then it came—a swift series of simple feints that were muscle flashes. Cannam was dazzled. So was the audience. No two of the onlookers could agree afterward as to what took place. Cannam ducked one feint and at the same time threw up his face guard to meet another feint for his jaw. He also attempted to change position with his legs. Ring-side witnesses swore that they saw Glendon start the blow from his right hip and leap forward like a tiger to add the weight of his body to it. Be that as it may, the blow caught Cannam on the point of the chin at the moment of his shift of position. And like Hanford, he was unconscious in the air before he struck the ropes and fell through on the heads of the reporters.

Of what happened afterward that night in the Golden Gate Arena, columns in the newspapers were unable adequately to describe. The police kept the ring clear, but they could not save the Arena. It was not a riot. It was an orgy. Not a seat was left standing. All over the great hall, by main strength, crowding and jostling to lay hands on beams and boards, the crowd uprooted and over-turned. Prize-fighters sought protection of the police, but there were not enough police to escort them out, and fighters, managers, and promoters were beaten and battered. Jim Hanford alone was spared. His jaw, prodigiously swollen, earned him this mercy. Outside, when finally driven from the building, the crowd fell upon a new seven-thousand-dollar motor car belonging to a well-known fight promoter and reduced it to scrapiron and kindling wood.

Glendon, unable to dress amid the wreckage of dressing rooms, gained his automobile, still in his ring costume and wrapped in a bath robe, but failed to escape. By weight of numbers the crowd caught and held his machine. The police were too busy to rescue him, and in the end a compromise was effected, whereby the car was permitted to proceed at a walk escorted by five thousand cheering madmen.

It was midnight when this storm swept past Union Square and down upon the St. Francis. Cries for a speech went up, and though at the hotel entrance, Glendon was good-naturedly restrained from escaping. He even tried leaping out upon the heads of the enthusiasts, but his feet never touched the pavement. On heads and shoulders, clutched at and uplifted by every hand that could touch his body, he went back through the air to the machine. Then he gave his speech, and Maud Glendon, looking down from an upper window at her young Hercules towering on the seat of the automobile, knew, as she always knew, that he meant it when he repeated that he had fought his last fight and retired from the ring forever.

The End

82

CHRIS FARRINGTON: ABLE SEAMAN

"If you vas in der old country ships, a liddle shaver like you vood pe only der boy, und you vood wait on der able seamen. Und ven der able seaman sing out, 'Boy, der water-jug!' you vood jump quick, like a shot, und bring der water-jug. Und ven der able seaman sing out, 'Boy, my boots!' you vood get der boots. Und you vood pe politeful, und say 'Yessir' und 'No sir.' But you pe in der American ship, and you t'ink you are so good as der able seamen. Chris, mine boy, I haf ben a sailorman for twenty-two years, und do you t'ink you are so good as me? I vas a sailorman pefore you vas borned, und I knot und reef und splice ven you play mit topstrings und fly kites."

"But you are unfair, Emil!" cried Chris Farrington, his sensitive face flushed and hurt. He was a slender though strongly built young fellow of seventeen, with Yankee ancestry writ large all over him.

"Dere you go vonce again!" the Swedish sailor exploded. "My name is Mister Johansen, und a kid of a boy like you call me 'Emil!' It vas insulting, und comes pecause of der American ship!"

"But you call me 'Chris'!" the boy expostulated, reproachfully.

"But you vas a boy."

"Who does a man's work," Chris retorted. "And because I do a man's work I have as much right to call you by your first name as

83

you me. We are all equals in this fo'castle, and you know it. When we signed for the voyage in San Francisco, we signed as sailors on the Sophie Sutherland and there was no difference made with any of us. Haven't I always done my work? Did I ever shirk? Did you or any other man ever have to take a wheel for me? Or a lookout? Or go aloft?"

"Chris is right," interrupted a young English sailor. "No man has had to do a tap of his work yet. He signed as good as any of us and he's shown himself as good—"

"Better!" broke in a Novia Scotia man. "Better than some of us! When we struck the sealing-grounds he turned out to be next to the best boat-steerer aboard. Only French Louis, who'd been at it for years, could beat him. I'm only a boat-puller, and you're only a boat-puller, too, Emil Johansen, for all your twenty-two years at sea. Why don't you become a boat-steerer?"

"Too clumsy," laughed the Englishman, "and too slow."

"Little that counts, one way or the other," joined in Dane Jurgensen, coming to the aid of his Scandinavian brother. "Emil is a man grown and an able seaman; the boy is neither."

And so the argument raged back and forth, the Swedes, Norwegians and Danes, because of race kinship, taking the part of Johansen, and the English, Canadians and Americans taking the part of Chris. From an unprejudiced point of view, the right was on the side of Chris. As he had truly said, he did a man's work, and the same work that any of them did. But they were prejudiced, and badly so, and out of the words which passed rose a standing quarrel which divided the forecastle into two parties.

The Sophie Sutherland was a seal-hunter, registered out of San

Francisco, and engaged in hunting the furry sea-animals along the Japanese coast north to Bering Sea. The other vessels were two-masted schooners, but she was a three-master and the largest in the fleet. In fact, she was a full-rigged, three-topmast schooner, newly built.

Although Chris Farrington knew that justice was with him, and that he performed all his work faithfully and well, many a time, in secret thought, he longed for some pressing emergency to arise whereby he could demonstrate to the Scandinavian seamen that he also was an able seaman.

But one stormy night, by an accident for which he was in nowise accountable, in overhauling a spare anchor-chain he had all the fingers of his left hand badly crushed. And his hopes were likewise crushed, for it was impossible for him to continue hunting with the boats, and he was forced to stay idly aboard until his fingers should heal. Yet, although he little dreamed it, this very accident was to give him the long-looked-for-opportunity.

One afternoon in the latter part of May the Sophie Sutherland rolled sluggishly in a breathless calm. The seals were abundant, the hunting good, and the boats were all away and out of sight. And with them was almost every man of the crew. Besides Chris, there remained only the captain, the sailing-master and the Chinese cook.

The captain was captain only by courtesy. He was an old man, past eighty, and blissfully ignorant of the sea and its ways; but he was the owner of the vessel, and hence the honorable title. Of course the sailing-master, who was really captain, was a thorough-going seaman. The mate, whose post was aboard, was out with the boats, having temporarily taken Chris's place as boat-steerer.

85

When good weather and good sport came together, the boats were accustomed to range far and wide, and often did not return to the schooner until long after dark. But for all that it was a perfect hunting day, Chris noted a growing anxiety on the part of the sailing-master. He paced the deck nervously, and was constantly sweeping the horizon with his marine glasses. Not a boat was in sight. As sunset arrived, he even sent Chris aloft to the mizzen-topmast-head, but with no better luck. The boats could not possibly be back before midnight.

Since noon the barometer had been falling with startling rapidity, and all the signs were ripe for a great storm—how great, not even the sailing-master anticipated. He and Chris set to work to prepare for it. They put storm gaskets on the furled topsails, lowered and stowed the foresail and spanker and took in the two inner jibs. In the one remaining jib they put a single reef, and a single reef in the mainsail.

Night had fallen before they finished, and with the darkness came the storm. A low moan swept over the sea, and the wind struck the Sophie Sutherland flat. But she righted quickly, and with the sailing-master at the wheel, sheered her bow into within five points of the wind. Working as well as he could with his bandaged hand, and with the feeble aid of the Chinese cook, Chris went forward and backed the jib over to the weather side. This with the flat mainsail, left the schooner hove to.

"God help the boats! It's no gale! It's a typhoon!" the sailing-master shouted to Chris at eleven o'clock. "Too much canvas! Got to get two more reefs into the mainsail, and got to do it right away!" He glanced at the old captain, shivering in oilskins at the binnacle and holding on for dear life. "There's only you and I, Chris—and the cook; but he's next to worthless!"

In order to make the reef, it was necessary to lower the mainsail, and the removal of this after pressure was bound to make the schooner fall off before the wind and sea because of the forward pressure of the jib.

"Take the wheel!" the sailing-master directed. "And when I give the word, hard up with it! And when she's square before it, steady her! And keep her there! We'll heave to again as soon as I get the reefs in!"

Gripping the kicking spokes, Chris watched him and the reluctant cook go forward into the howling darkness. The Sophie Sutherland was plunging into the huge head-seas and wallowing tremendously, the tense steel stays and taut rigging humming like harp-strings to the wind. A buffeted cry came to his ears, and he felt the schooner's bow paying off of its own accord. The mainsail was down!

He ran the wheel hard-over and kept anxious track of the changing direction of the wind on his face and of the heave of the vessel. This was the crucial moment. In performing the evolution she would have to pass broadside to the surge before she could get before it. The wind was blowing directly on his right cheek, when he felt the Sophie Sutherland lean over and begin to rise toward the sky— up—up—an infinite distance! Would she clear the crest of the gigantic wave?

Again by the feel of it, for he could see nothing, he knew that a wall of water was rearing and curving far above him along the whole weather side. There was an instant's calm as the liquid wall intervened and shut off the wind. The schooner righted, and for that instant seemed at perfect rest. Then she rolled to meet the descending rush.

87

Chris shouted to the captain to hold tight, and prepared himself for the shock. But the man did not live who could face it. An ocean of water smote Chris's back and his clutch on the spokes was loosened as if it were a baby's. Stunned, powerless, like a straw on the face of a torrent, he was swept onward he knew not whither. Missing the corner of the cabin, he was dashed forward along the poop runway a hundred feet or more, striking violently against the foot of the foremast. A second wave, crushing inboard, hurled him back the way he had come, and left him half-drowned where the poop steps should have been.

Bruised and bleeding, dimly conscious, he felt for the rail and dragged himself to his feet. Unless something could be done, he knew the last moment had come. As he faced the poop, the wind drove into his mouth with suffocating force. This brought him back to his senses with a start. The wind was blowing from dead aft! The schooner was out of the trough and before it! But the send of the sea was bound to breach her to again. Crawling up the runway, he managed to get to the wheel just in time to prevent this. The binnacle light was still burning. They were safe!

That is, he and the schooner were safe. As to the welfare of his three companions he could not say. Nor did he dare leave the wheel in order to find out, for it took every second of his undivided attention to keep the vessel to her course. The least fraction of carelessness and the heave of the sea under the quarter was liable to thrust her into the trough. So, a boy of one hundred and forty pounds, he clung to his herculean task of guiding the two hundred straining tons of fabric amid the chaos of the great storm forces.

Half an hour later, groaning and sobbing, the captain crawled to Chris's feet. All was lost, he whimpered. He was smitten unto death. The galley had gone by the board, the mainsail and running-gear, the cook, every thing!

"Where's the sailing-master?" Chris demanded when he had caught his breath after steadying a wild lurch of the schooner. It was no child's play to steer a vessel under single reefed jib before a typhoon.

"Clean up for'ard," the old man replied "Jammed under the fo'c'sle-head, but still breathing. Both his arms are broken, he says and he doesn't know how many ribs. He's hurt bad."

"Well, he'll drown there the way she's shipping water through the hawse-pipes. Go for'ard!" Chris commanded, taking charge of things as a matter of course. "Tell him not to worry; that I'm at the wheel. Help him as much as you can, and make him help"—he stopped and ran the spokes to starboard as a tremendous billow rose under the stern and yawed the schooner to port—"and make him help himself for the rest. Unship the fo'castle hatch and get him down into a bunk. Then ship the hatch again."

The captain turned his aged face forward and wavered pitifully. The waist of the ship was full of water to the bulwarks. He had just come through it, and knew death lurked every inch of the way.

"Go!" Chris shouted, fiercely. And as the fear-stricken man started, "And take another look for the cook!"

Two hours later, almost dead from suffering, the captain returned. He had obeyed orders. The sailing-master was helpless, although safe in a bunk; the cook was gone. Chris sent the captain below to the cabin to change his clothes.

After interminable hours of toil day broke cold and gray. Chris

89

looked about him. The Sophie Sutherland was racing before the typhoon like a thing possessed. There was no rain, but the wind whipped the spray of the sea mast-high, obscuring everything except in the immediate neighborhood.

Two waves only could Chris see at a time—the one before and the one behind. So small and insignificant the schooner seemed on the long Pacific roll! Rushing up a maddening mountain, she would poise like a cockle-shell on the giddy summit, breathless and rolling, leap outward and down into the yawning chasm beneath, and bury herself in the smother of foam at the bottom. Then the recovery, another mountain, another sickening upward rush, another poise, and the downward crash. Abreast of him, to starboard, like a ghost of the storm, Chris saw the cook dashing apace with the schooner. Evidently, when washed overboard, he had grasped and become entangled in a trailing halyard.

For three hours more, alone with this gruesome companion, Chris held the Sophie Sutherland before the wind and sea. He had long since forgotten his mangled fingers. The bandages had been torn away, and the cold, salt spray had eaten into the half-healed wounds until they were numb and no longer pained. But he was not cold. The terrific labor of steering forced the perspiration from every pore. Yet he was faint and weak with hunger and exhaustion, and hailed with delight the advent on deck of the captain, who fed him all of a pound of cake-chocolate. It strengthened him at once.

He ordered the captain to cut the halyard by which the cook's body was towing, and also to go forward and cut loose the jib-halyard and sheet. When he had done so, the jib fluttered a couple of moments like a handkerchief, then tore out of the bolt-ropes and vanished. The Sophie Sutherland was running under bare poles.

By noon the storm had spent itself, and by six in the evening the waves had died down sufficiently to let Chris leave the helm. It was almost hopeless to dream of the small boats weathering the typhoon, but there is always the chance in saving human life, and Chris at once applied himself to going back over the course along which he had fled. He managed to get a reef in one of the inner jibs and two reefs in the spanker, and then, with the aid of the watch-tackle, to hoist them to the stiff breeze that yet blew. And all through the night, tacking back and forth on the back track, he shook out canvas as fast as the wind would permit.

The injured sailing-master had turned delirious and between tending him and lending a hand with the ship, Chris kept the captain busy. "Taught me more seamanship," as he afterward said, "than I'd learned on the whole voyage." But by daybreak the old man's feeble frame succumbed, and he fell off into exhausted sleep on the weather poop.

Chris, who could now lash the wheel, covered the tired man with blankets from below, and went fishing in the lazaretto for something to eat. But by the day following he found himself forced to give in, drowsing fitfully by the wheel and waking ever and anon to take a look at things.

On the afternoon of the third day he picked up a schooner, dismasted and battered. As he approached, close-hauled on the wind, he saw her decks crowded by an unusually large crew, and on sailing in closer, made out among others the faces of his missing comrades. And he was just in the nick of time, for they were fighting a losing fight at the pumps. An hour later they, with the crew of the sinking craft were aboard the Sophie Sutherland.

Having wandered so far from their own vessel, they had taken

91

refuge on the strange schooner just before the storm broke. She was a Canadian sealer on her first voyage, and as was now apparent, her last.

The captain of the Sophie Sutherland had a story to tell, also, and he told it well—so well, in fact, that when all hands were gathered together on deck during the dog-watch, Emil Johansen strode over to Chris and gripped him by the hand.

"Chris," he said, so loudly that all could hear, "Chris, I gif in. You vas yoost so good a sailorman as I. You vas a bully boy und able seaman, und I pe proud for you!

"Und Chris!" He turned as if he had forgotten something, and called back, "From dis time always you call me 'Emil' mitout der 'Mister'!"

TYPHOON OFF THE COAST OF JAPAN

Jack London's First Story, Published at the Age of Seventeen.

It was four bells in the morning watch. We had just finished breakfast when the order came forward for the watch on deck to stand by to heave her to and all hands stand by the boats.

"Port! hard a port!" cried our sailing-master. "Clew up the topsails! Let the flying jib run down! Back the jib over to windward and run down the foresail!" And so was our schooner Sophie Sutherland hove to off the Japan coast, near Cape Jerimo, on April 10, 1893.

Then came moments of bustle and confusion. There were eighteen men to man the six boats. Some were hooking on the falls, others casting off the lashings; boat-steerers appeared with boat-compasses and water-breakers, and boat-pullers with the lunch boxes. Hunters were staggering under two or three shotguns, a rifle and heavy ammunition box, all of which were soon stowed away with their oilskins and mittens in the boats.

The sailing-master gave his last orders, and away we went, pulling three pairs of oars to gain our positions. We were in the weather boat, and so had a longer pull than the others. The first, second and third lee boats soon had all sail set and were running off to the southward and westward with the wind beam, while the schooner was running off to leeward of them, so that in case of accident the boats would have fair wind home.

It was a glorious morning, but our boat steerer shook his head ominously as he glanced at the rising sun and prophetically muttered: "Red sun in the morning, sailor take warning." The sun

93

had an angry look, and a few light, fleecy "nigger-heads" in that quarter seemed abashed and frightened and soon disappeared.

Away off to the northward Cape Jerimo reared its black, forbidding head like some huge monster rising from the deep. The winter's snow, not yet entirely dissipated by the sun, covered it in patches of glistening white, over which the light wind swept on its way out to sea. Huge gulls rose slowly, fluttering their wings in the light breeze and striking their webbed feet on the surface of the water for over half a mile before they could leave it. Hardly had the patter, patter died away when a flock of sea quail rose, and with whistling wings flew away to windward, where members of a large band of whales were disporting themselves, their blowings sounding like the exhaust of steam engines. The harsh, discordant cries of a sea-parrot grated unpleasantly on the ear, and set half a dozen alert in a small band of seals that were ahead of us. Away they went, breaching and jumping entirely out of water. A sea-gull with slow, deliberate flight and long, majestic curves circled round us, and as a reminder of home a little English sparrow perched impudently on the fo'castle head, and, cocking his head on one side, chirped merrily. The boats were soon among the seals, and the bang! bang! of the guns could be heard from down to leeward.

The wind was slowly rising, and by three o'clock as, with a dozen seals in our boat, we were deliberating whether to go on or turn back, the recall flag was run up at the schooner's mizzen—a sure sign that with the rising wind the barometer was falling and that our sailing-master was getting anxious for the welfare of the boats.

Away we went before the wind with a single reef in our sail. With clenched teeth sat the boat-steerer, grasping the steering oar firmly with both hands, his restless eyes on the alert—a glance at the schooner ahead, as we rose on a sea, another at the mainsheet, and then one astern where the dark ripple of the wind on the water told him of a coming puff or a large white-cap that threatened to overwhelm us. The waves were holding high carnival, performing the strangest antics, as with wild glee they danced along in fierce pursuit—now up, now down, here, there, and everywhere, until some great sea of liquid green with its milk-white crest of foam rose from the ocean's throbbing bosom and drove the others from view. But only for a moment, for again under new forms they reappeared. In the sun's path they wandered, where every ripple, great or small, every little spit or spray looked like molten silver, where the water lost its dark green color and became a dazzling, silvery flood, only to vanish and become a wild waste of sullen turbulence, each dark foreboding sea rising and breaking, then rolling on again. The dash, the sparkle, the silvery light soon vanished with the sun, which became obscured by black clouds that were rolling swiftly in from the west, northwest; apt heralds of the coming storm.

We soon reached the schooner and found ourselves the last aboard. In a few minutes the seals were skinned, boats and decks washed, and we were down below by the roaring fo'castle fire, with a wash, change of clothes, and a hot, substantial supper before us. Sail had been put on the schooner, as we had a run of seventy-five miles to make to the southward before morning, so as to get in the midst of the seals, out of which we had strayed during the last two days' hunting.

We had the first watch from eight to midnight. The wind was soon blowing half a gale, and our sailing-master expected little sleep that night as he paced up and down the poop. The topsails were soon clewed up and made fast, then the flying jib run down and furled. Quite a sea was rolling by this time, occasionally breaking over the decks, flooding them and threatening to smash the boats. At six bells we were ordered to turn them over and put on storm lashings. This occupied us till eight bells, when we were relieved by the mid-watch. I was the last to go below, doing so just as the watch on deck was furling the spanker. Below all were asleep except our green hand, the "bricklayer," who was dying of consumption. The wildly dancing movements of the sea lamp cast a pale, flickering light through the fo'castle and turned to golden honey the drops of water on the yellow oilskins. In all the corners dark shadows seemed to come and go, while up in the eyes of her, beyond the pall bits, descending from deck to deck, where they seemed to lurk like some dragon at the cavern's mouth, it was dark as Erebus. Now and again, the light seemed to penetrate for a moment as the schooner rolled heavier than usual, only to recede, leaving it darker and blacker than before. The roar of the wind through the rigging came to the ear muffled like the distant rumble of a train crossing a trestle or the surf on the beach, while the loud crash of the seas on her weather bow seemed almost to rend the beams and planking asunder as it resounded through the fo'castle. The creaking and groaning of the timbers, stanchions, and bulkheads, as the strain the vessel was undergoing was felt, served to drown the groans of the dying man as he tossed uneasily in his bunk. The working of the foremast against the deck beams caused a shower of flaky powder to fall, and sent another sound mingling with the tumultuous storm. Small cascades of water streamed from the pall bits from the fo'castle head above, and, joining issue with the streams from the wet oilskins, ran along the floor and disappeared aft into the main hold.

At two bells in the middle watch—that is, in land parlance one o'clock in the morning;—the order was roared out on the fo'castle: "All hands on deck and shorten sail!"

Then the sleepy sailors tumbled out of their bunk and into their clothes, oilskins and sea-boots and up on deck. 'Tis when that order comes on cold, blustering nights that "Jack" grimly mutters: "Who would not sell a farm and go to sea?"

It was on deck that the force of the wind could be fully appreciated, especially after leaving the stifling fo'castle. It seemed to stand up against you like a wall, making it almost impossible to move on the heaving decks or to breathe as the fierce gusts came dashing by. The schooner was hove to under jib, foresail and mainsail. We proceeded to lower the foresail and make it fast. The night was dark, greatly impeding our labor. Still, though not a star or the moon could pierce the black masses of storm clouds that obscured the sky as they swept along before the gale, nature aided us in a measure. A soft light emanated from the movement of the ocean. Each mighty sea, all phosphorescent and glowing with the tiny lights of myriads of animalculae, threatened to overwhelm us with a deluge of fire. Higher and higher, thinner and thinner, the crest grew as it began to curve and overtop preparatory to breaking, until with a roar it fell over the bulwarks, a mass of soft glowing light and tons of water which sent the sailors sprawling in all directions and left in each nook and cranny little specks of light that glowed and trembled till the next sea washed them away, depositing new ones in their places. Sometimes several seas following each other with great rapidity and thundering down on our decks filled them full to the bulwarks, but soon they were discharged through the lee scuppers.

To reef the mainsail we were forced to run off before the gale under the single reefed jib. By the time we had finished the wind had forced up such a tremendous sea that it was impossible to heave her to. Away we flew on the wings of the storm through the muck and flying spray. A wind sheer to starboard, then another to port as the enormous seas struck the schooner astern and nearly broached her to. As day broke we took in the jib, leaving not a sail unfurled. Since we had begun scudding she had ceased to take the seas over her bow, but amidships they broke fast and furious. It was a dry storm in the matter of rain, but the force of the wind filled the air with fine spray, which flew as high as the crosstrees and cut the face like a knife, making it impossible to see over a hundred yards ahead. The sea was a dark lead color as with long, slow, majestic roll it was heaped up by the wind into liquid mountains of foam. The wild antics of the schooner were sickening as she forged along. She would almost stop, as though climbing a mountain, then rapidly rolling to right and left as she gained the summit of a huge sea, she steadied herself and paused for a moment as though affrighted at the yawning precipice before her. Like an avalanche, she shot forward and down as the sea astern struck her with the force of a thousand battering rams, burying her bow to the cat-heads in the milky foam at the bottom that came on deck in all directions—forward, astern, to right and left, through the hawse-pipes and over the rail.

The wind began to drop, and by ten o'clock we were talking of heaving her to. We passed a ship, two schooners and a four-masted barkentine under the smallest canvas, and at eleven o'clock, running up the spanker and jib, we hove her to, and in another hour we were beating back again against the aftersea under full sail to regain the sealing ground away to the westward.

Below, a couple of men were sewing the "bricklayer's" body in canvas preparatory to the sea burial. And so with the storm passed away the "bricklayer's" soul.

THE LOST POACHER

"But they won't take excuses. You're across the line, and that's enough. They'll take you. In you go, Siberia and the salt mines. And as for Uncle Sam, why, what's he to know about it? Never a word will get back to the States. 'The Mary Thomas,' the papers will say, 'the Mary Thomas lost with all hands. Probably in a typhoon in the Japanese seas.' That's what the papers will say, and people, too. In you go, Siberia and the salt mines. Dead to the world and kith and kin, though you live fifty years."

In such manner John Lewis, commonly known as the "sea-lawyer," settled the matter out of hand.

It was a serious moment in the forecastle of the Mary Thomas. No sooner had the watch below begun to talk the trouble over, than the watch on deck came down and joined them. As there was no wind, every hand could be spared with the exception of the man at the wheel, and he remained only for the sake of discipline. Even "Bub" Russell, the cabin-boy, had crept forward to hear what was going on.

However, it was a serious moment, as the grave faces of the sailors bore witness. For the three preceding months the Mary Thomas sealing schooner, had hunted the seal pack along the coast of Japan and north to Bering Sea. Here, on the Asiatic side of the sea, they were forced to give over the chase, or rather, to go no farther; for beyond, the Russian cruisers patrolled forbidden ground, where the seals might breed in peace.

A week before she had fallen into a heavy fog accompanied by calm. Since then the fog-bank had not lifted, and the only wind had been light airs and catspaws. This in itself was not so bad, for the sealing schooners are never in a hurry so long as they are in the midst of the seals; but the trouble lay in the fact that the current at this point bore heavily to the north. Thus the Mary Thomas had unwittingly drifted across the line, and every hour she was penetrating, unwillingly, farther and farther into the dangerous waters where the Russian bear kept guard.

How far she had drifted no man knew. The sun had not been visible for a week, nor the stars, and the captain had been unable to take observations in order to determine his position. At any moment a cruiser might swoop down and hale the crew away to Siberia. The fate of other poaching seal-hunters was too well known to the men of the Mary Thomas, and there was cause for grave faces.

"Mine friends," spoke up a German boat-steerer, "it vas a pad piziness. Shust as ve make a big catch, und all honest, somedings go wrong, und der Russians nab us, dake our skins and our schooner, und send us mit der anarchists to Siberia. Ach! a pretty pad piziness!"

"Yes, that's where it hurts," the sea lawyer went on. "Fifteen hundred skins in the salt piles, and all honest, a big pay-day coming to every man Jack of us, and then to be captured and lose it all! It'd be different if we'd been poaching, but it's all honest work in open water."

"But if we haven't done anything wrong, they can't do anything to us, can they?" Bub queried.

"It strikes me as 'ow it ain't the proper thing for a boy o' your age shovin' in when 'is elders is talkin'," protested an English sailor, from over the edge of his bunk.

100

"Oh, that's all right, Jack," answered the sea-lawyer. "He's a perfect right to. Ain't he just as liable to lose his wages as the rest of us?"

"Wouldn't give thruppence for them!" Jack sniffed back. He had been planning to go home and see his family in Chelsea when he was paid off, and he was now feeling rather blue over the highly possible loss, not only of his pay, but of his liberty.

"How are they to know?" the sea-lawyer asked in answer to Bub's previous question. "Here we are in forbidden water. How do they know but what we came here of our own accord? Here we are, fifteen hundred skins in the hold. How do they know whether we got them in open water or in the closed sea? Don't you see, Bub, the evidence is all against us. If you caught a man with his pockets full of apples like those which grow on your tree, and if you caught him in your tree besides, what'd you think if he told you he couldn't help it, and had just been sort of blown there, and that anyway those apples came from some other tree—what'd you think, eh?"

Bub saw it clearly when put in that light, and shook his head despondently.

"You'd rather be dead than go to Siberia," one of the boat-pullers said. "They put you into the salt-mines and work you till you die. Never see daylight again. Why, I've heard tell of one fellow that was chained to his mate, and that mate died. And they were both chained together! And if they send you to the quicksilver mines you get salivated. I'd rather be hung than salivated."

"Wot's salivated?" Jack asked, suddenly sitting up in his bunk at the hint of fresh misfortunes.

"Why, the quicksilver gets into your blood; I think that's the way. And your gums all swell like you had the scurvy, only worse, and

101

your teeth get loose in your jaws. And big ulcers forms, and then you die horrible. The strongest man can't last long a-mining quicksilver."

"A pad piziness," the boat-steerer reiterated, dolorously, in the silence which followed. "A pad piziness. I vish I vas in Yokohama. Eh? Vot vas dot?"

The vessel had suddenly heeled over. The decks were aslant. A tin pannikin rolled down the inclined plane, rattling and banging. From above came the slapping of canvas and the quivering rat-tat-tat of the after leech of the loosely stretched foresail. Then the mate's voice sang down the hatch, "All hands on deck and make sail!"

Never had such summons been answered with more enthusiasm. The calm had broken. The wind had come which was to carry them south into safety. With a wild cheer all sprang on deck. Working with mad haste, they flung out topsails, flying jibs and staysails. As they worked, the fog-bank lifted and the black vault of heaven, bespangled with the old familiar stars, rushed into view. When all was shipshape, the Mary Thomas was lying gallantly over on her side to a beam wind and plunging ahead due south.

"Steamer's lights ahead on the port bow, sir!" cried the lookout from his station on the forecastle-head. There was excitement in the man's voice.

The captain sent Bub below for his night-glasses. Everybody crowded to the lee-rail to gaze at the suspicious stranger, which already began to loom up vague and indistinct. In those unfrequented waters the chance was one in a thousand that it could be anything else than a Russian patrol. The captain was still anxiously gazing through the glasses, when a flash of flame left the stranger's side, followed by the loud report of a cannon. The worst fears were confirmed. It was a patrol, evidently firing across the bows of the Mary Thomas in order to make her heave to.

"Hard down with your helm!" the captain commanded the steersman, all the life gone out of his voice. Then to the crew, "Back over the jib and foresail! Run down the flying jib! Clew up the foretopsail! And aft here and swing on to the main-sheet!"

The Mary Thomas ran into the eye of the wind, lost headway, and fell to courtesying gravely to the long seas rolling up from the west.

The cruiser steamed a little nearer and lowered a boat. The sealers watched in heartbroken silence. They could see the white bulk of the boat as it was slacked away to the water, and its crew sliding aboard. They could hear the creaking of the davits and the commands of the officers. Then the boat sprang away under the impulse of the oars, and came toward them. The wind had been rising, and already the sea was too rough to permit the frail craft to lie alongside the tossing schooner; but watching their chance, and taking advantage of the boarding ropes thrown to them, an officer and a couple of men clambered aboard. The boat then sheered off into safety and lay to its oars, a young midshipman, sitting in the stern and holding the yoke-lines, in charge.

The officer, whose uniform disclosed his rank as that of second lieutenant in the Russian navy went below with the captain of the Mary Thomas to look at the ship's papers. A few minutes later he emerged, and upon his sailors removing the hatch-covers, passed down into the hold with a lantern to inspect the salt piles. It was a goodly heap which confronted him—fifteen hundred fresh skins, the season's catch; and under the circumstances he could have had but one conclusion.

103

"I am very sorry," he said, in broken English to the sealing captain, when he again came on deck, "but it is my duty, in the name of the tsar, to seize your vessel as a poacher caught with fresh skins in the closed sea. The penalty, as you may know, is confiscation and imprisonment."

The captain of the Mary Thomas shrugged his shoulders in seeming indifference, and turned away. Although they may restrain all outward show, strong men, under unmerited misfortune, are sometimes very close to tears. Just then the vision of his little California home, and of the wife and two yellow-haired boys, was strong upon him, and there was a strange, choking sensation in his throat, which made him afraid that if he attempted to speak he would sob instead.

And also there was upon him the duty he owed his men. No weakness before them, for he must be a tower of strength to sustain them in misfortune. He had already explained to the second lieutenant, and knew the hopelessness of the situation. As the sea-lawyer had said, the evidence was all against him. So he turned aft, and fell to pacing up and down the poop of the vessel over which he was no longer commander.

The Russian officer now took temporary charge. He ordered more of his men aboard, and had all the canvas clewed up and furled snugly away. While this was being done, the boat plied back and forth between the two vessels, passing a heavy hawser, which was made fast to the great towing-bitts on the schooner's forecastle-head. During all this work the sealers stood about in sullen groups. It was madness to think of resisting, with the guns of a man-of-war not a biscuit-toss away; but they refused to lend a hand, preferring instead to maintain a gloomy silence.

Having accomplished his task, the lieutenant ordered all but four of his men back into the boat. Then the midshipman, a lad of sixteen, looking strangely mature and dignified in his uniform and sword, came aboard to take command of the captured sealer. Just as the lieutenant prepared to depart his eye chanced to alight upon Bub. Without a word of warning, he seized him by the arm and dropped him over the rail into the waiting boat; and then, with a parting wave of his hand, he followed him.

It was only natural that Bub should be frightened at this unexpected happening. All the terrible stories he had heard of the Russians served to make him fear them, and now returned to his mind with double force. To be captured by them was bad enough, but to be carried off by them, away from his comrades, was a fate of which he had not dreamed.

"Be a good boy, Bub," the captain called to him, as the boat drew away from the Mary Thomas's side, "and tell the truth!"

"Aye, aye, sir!" he answered, bravely enough by all outward appearance. He felt a certain pride of race, and was ashamed to be a coward before these strange enemies, these wild Russian bears.

"Und be politeful!" the German boat-steerer added, his rough voice lifting across the water like a fog-horn.

Bub waved his hand in farewell, and his mates clustered along the rail as they answered with a cheering shout. He found room in the stern-sheets, where he fell to regarding the lieutenant. He didn't look so wild or bearish after all—very much like other men, Bub concluded, and the sailors were much the same as all other man-of-war's men he had ever known. Nevertheless, as his feet struck the steel deck of the cruiser, he felt as if he had entered the portals of a prison.

For a few minutes he was left unheeded. The sailors hoisted the boat up, and swung it in on the davits. Then great clouds of black smoke poured out of the funnels, and they were under way—to Siberia, Bub could not help but think. He saw the Mary Thomas swing abruptly into line as she took the pressure from the hawser, and her side-lights, red and green, rose and fell as she was towed through the sea.

Bub's eyes dimmed at the melancholy sight, but—but just then the lieutenant came to take him down to the commander, and he straightened up and set his lips firmly, as if this were a very commonplace affair and he were used to being sent to Siberia every day in the week. The cabin in which the commander sat was like a palace compared to the humble fittings of the Mary Thomas, and the commander himself, in gold lace and dignity, was a most august personage, quite unlike the simple man who navigated his schooner on the trail of the seal pack.

Bub now quickly learned why he had been brought aboard, and in the prolonged questioning which followed, told nothing but the plain truth. The truth was harmless; only a lie could have injured his cause. He did not know much, except that they had been sealing far to the south in open water, and that when the calm and fog came down upon them, being close to the line, they had drifted across. Again and again he insisted that they had not lowered a boat or shot a seal in the week they had been drifting about in the forbidden sea; but the commander chose to consider all that he said to be a tissue of falsehoods, and adopted a bullying tone in an effort to frighten the boy. He threatened and cajoled by turns, but failed in the slightest to shake Bub's statements, and at last ordered him out of his presence.

By some oversight, Bub was not put in anybody's charge, and

wandered up on deck unobserved. Sometimes the sailors, in passing, bent curious glances upon him, but otherwise he was left strictly alone. Nor could he have attracted much attention, for he was small, the night dark, and the watch on deck intent on its own business. Stumbling over the strange decks, he made his way aft where he could look upon the side-lights of the Mary Thomas, following steadily in the rear.

For a long while he watched, and then lay down in the darkness close to where the hawser passed over the stern to the captured schooner. Once an officer came up and examined the straining rope to see if it were chafing, but Bub cowered away in the shadow undiscovered. This, however, gave him an idea which concerned the lives and liberties of twenty-two men, and which was to avert crushing sorrow from more than one happy home many thousand miles away.

In the first place, he reasoned, the crew were all guiltless of any crime, and yet were being carried relentlessly away to imprisonment in Siberia—a living death, he had heard, and he believed it implicitly. In the second place, he was a prisoner, hard and fast, with no chance to escape. In the third, it was possible for the twenty-two men on the Mary Thomas to escape. The only thing which bound them was a four-inch hawser. They dared not cut it at their end, for a watch was sure to be maintained upon it by their Russian captors; but at this end, ah! at his end—

Bub did not stop to reason further. Wriggling close to the hawser, he opened his jack-knife and went to work. The blade was not very sharp, and he sawed away, rope-yarn by rope-yarn, the awful picture of the solitary Siberian exile he must endure growing clearer and more terrible at every stroke. Such a fate was bad enough to undergo with one's comrades, but to face it alone seemed frightful.

107

And besides, the very act he was performing was sure to bring greater punishment upon him.

In the midst of such somber thoughts, he heard footsteps approaching. He wriggled away into the shadow. An officer stopped where he had been working, half-stooped to examine the hawser, then changed his mind and straightened up. For a few minutes he stood there, gazing at the lights of the captured schooner, and then went forward again.

Now was the time! Bub crept back and went on sawing. Now two parts were severed. Now three. But one remained. The tension upon this was so great that it readily yielded. Splash the freed end went overboard. He lay quietly, his heart in his mouth, listening. No one on the cruiser but himself had heard.

He saw the red and green lights of the Mary Thomas grow dimmer and dimmer. Then a faint hallo came over the water from the Russian prize crew. Still nobody heard. The smoke continued to pour out of the cruiser's funnels, and her propellers throbbed as mightily as ever.

What was happening on the Mary Thomas? Bub could only surmise; but of one thing he was certain: his comrades would assert themselves and overpower the four sailors and the midshipman. A few minutes later he saw a small flash, and straining his ears heard the very faint report of a pistol. Then, oh joy! both the red and green lights suddenly disappeared. The Mary Thomas was retaken!

Just as an officer came aft, Bub crept forward, and hid away in one of the boats. Not an instant too soon. The alarm was given. Loud voices rose in command. The cruiser altered her course. An electric search-light began to throw its white rays across the sea, here, there,

108

everywhere; but in its flashing path no tossing schooner was revealed.

Bub went to sleep soon after that, nor did he wake till the gray of dawn. The engines were pulsing monotonously, and the water, splashing noisily, told him the decks were being washed down. One sweeping glance, and he saw that they were alone on the expanse of ocean. The Mary Thomas had escaped. As he lifted his head, a roar of laughter went up from the sailors. Even the officer, who ordered him taken below and locked up, could not quite conceal the laughter in his eyes. Bub thought often in the days of confinement which followed that they were not very angry with him for what he had done.

He was not far from right. There is a certain innate nobility deep down in the hearts of all men, which forces them to admire a brave act, even if it is performed by an enemy. The Russians were in nowise different from other men. True, a boy had outwitted them; but they could not blame him, and they were sore puzzled as to what to do with him. It would never do to take a little mite like him in to represent all that remained of the lost poacher.

So, two weeks later, a United States man-of-war, steaming out of the Russian port of Vladivostok, was signaled by a Russian cruiser. A boat passed between the two ships, and a small boy dropped over the rail upon the deck of the American vessel. A week later he was put ashore at Hakodate, and after some telegraphing, his fare was paid on the railroad to Yokohama.

From the depot he hurried through the quaint Japanese streets to the harbor, and hired a sampan boatman to put him aboard a certain vessel whose familiar rigging had quickly caught his eye. Her gaskets were off, her sails unfurled; she was just starting back

109

to the United States. As he came closer, a crowd of sailors sprang upon the forecastle head, and the windlass-bars rose and fell as the anchor was torn from its muddy bottom.

"'Yankee ship come down the ribber!'" the sea-lawyer's voice rolled out as he led the anchor song.

"'Pull, my bully boys, pull!'" roared back the old familiar chorus, the men's bodies lifting and bending to the rhythm.

Bub Russell paid the boatman and stepped on deck. The anchor was forgotten. A mighty cheer went up from the men, and almost before he could catch his breath he was on the shoulders of the captain, surrounded by his mates, and endeavoring to answer twenty questions to the second.

The next day a schooner hove to off a Japanese fishing village, sent ashore four sailors and a little midshipman, and sailed away. These men did not talk English, but they had money and quickly made their way to Yokohama. From that day the Japanese village folk never heard anything more about them, and they are still a much-talked-of mystery. As the Russian government never said anything about the incident, the United States is still ignorant of the whereabouts of the lost poacher, nor has she ever heard, officially, of the way in which some of her citizens "shanghaied" five subjects of the tsar. Even nations have secrets sometimes.

THE BANKS OF THE SACRAMENTO

"And it's blow, ye winds, heigh-ho,
For Cal-i-for-ni-o;
For there's plenty of gold so I've been told,
On the banks of the Sacramento!"

It was only a little boy, singing in a shrill treble the sea chantey which seamen sing the wide world over when they man the capstan bars and break the anchors out for "Frisco" port. It was only a little boy who had never seen the sea, but two hundred feet beneath him rolled the Sacramento. "Young" Jerry he was called, after "Old" Jerry, his father, from whom he had learned the song, as well as received his shock of bright-red hair, his blue, dancing eyes, and his fair and inevitably freckled skin.

For Old Jerry had been a sailor, and had followed the sea till middle life, haunted always by the words of the ringing chantey. Then one day he had sung the song in earnest, in an Asiatic port, swinging and thrilling round the capstan-circle with twenty others. And at San Francisco he turned his back upon his ship and upon the sea, and went to behold with his own eyes the banks of the Sacramento.

He beheld the gold, too, for he found employment at the Yellow Dream mine, and proved of utmost usefulness in rigging the great ore-cables across the river and two hundred feet above its surface.

After that he took charge of the cables and kept them in repair, and ran them and loved them, and became himself an indispensable fixture of the Yellow Dream mine. Then he loved pretty Margaret

111

Kelly; but she had left him and Young Jerry, the latter barely toddling, to take up her last long sleep in the little graveyard among the great sober pines.

Old Jerry never went back to the sea. He remained by his cables, and lavished upon them and Young Jerry all the love of his nature. When evil days came to the Yellow Dream, he still remained in the employ of the company as watchman over the all but abandoned property.

But this morning he was not visible. Young Jerry only was to be seen, sitting on the cabin step and singing the ancient chantey. He had cooked and eaten his breakfast all by himself, and had just come out to take a look at the world. Twenty feet before him stood the steel drum round which the endless cable worked. By the drum, snug and fast, was the ore-car. Following with his eyes the dizzy flight of the cables to the farther bank, he could see the other drum and the other car.

The contrivance was worked by gravity, the loaded car crossing the river by virtue of its own weight, and at the same time dragging the empty car back. The loaded car being emptied, and the empty car being loaded with more ore, the performance could be repeated—a performance which had been repeated tens of thousands of times since the day Old Jerry became the keeper of the cables.

Young Jerry broke off his song at the sound of approaching footsteps. A tall, blue-shirted man, a rifle across the hollow of his arm, came out from the gloom of the pine-trees. It was Hall, watchman of the Yellow Dragon mine, the cables of which spanned the Sacramento a mile farther up.

"Yello, younker!" was his greeting. "What you doin' here by your lonesome?"

"Oh, bachin'," Jerry tried to answer unconcernedly, as if it were a very ordinary sort of thing. "Dad's away, you see."

"Where's he gone?" the man asked.

"San Francisco. Went last night. His brother's dead in the old country, and he's gone down to see the lawyers. Won't be back till tomorrow night."

So spoke Jerry, and with pride, because of the responsibility which had fallen to him of keeping an eye on the property of the Yellow Dream, and the glorious adventure of living alone on the cliff above the river and of cooking his own meals.

"Well, take care of yourself," Hall said, "and don't monkey with the cables. I'm goin' to see if I can pick up a deer in the Cripple Cow Cañon."

"It's goin' to rain, I think," Jerry said, with mature deliberation.

"And it's little I mind a wettin'," Hall laughed, as he strode away among the trees.

Jerry's prediction concerning rain was more than fulfilled. By ten o'clock the pines were swaying and moaning, the cabin windows rattling, and the rain driving by in fierce squalls. At half past eleven he kindled a fire, and promptly at the stroke of twelve sat down to his dinner.

No out-of-doors for him that day, he decided, when he had washed the few dishes and put them neatly away; and he wondered how wet Hall was and whether he had succeeded in picking up a deer.

At one o'clock there came a knock at the door, and when he opened it a man and a woman staggered in on the breast of a great gust of

113

wind. They were Mr. and Mrs. Spillane, ranchers, who lived in a lonely valley a dozen miles back from the river.

"Where's Hall?" was Spillane's opening speech, and he spoke sharply and quickly.

Jerry noted that he was nervous and abrupt in his movements, and that Mrs. Spillane seemed laboring under some strong anxiety. She was a thin, washed-out, worked-out woman, whose life of dreary and unending toil had stamped itself harshly upon her face. It was the same life that had bowed her husband's shoulders and gnarled his hands and turned his hair to a dry and dusty gray.

"He's gone hunting up Cripple Cow," Jerry answered. "Did you want to cross?"

The woman began to weep quietly, while Spillane dropped a troubled exclamation and strode to the window. Jerry joined him in gazing out to where the cables lost themselves in the thick downpour.

It was the custom of the backwoods people in that section of country to cross the Sacramento on the Yellow Dragon cable. For this service a small toll was charged, which tolls the Yellow Dragon Company applied to the payment of Hall's wages.

"We've got to get across, Jerry," Spillane said, at the same time jerking his thumb over his shoulder in the direction of his wife. "Her father's hurt at the Clover Leaf. Powder explosion. Not expected to live. We just got word."

Jerry felt himself fluttering inwardly. He knew that Spillane wanted to cross on the Yellow Dream cable, and in the absence of his father he felt that he dared not assume such a responsibility, for the cable

114

had never been used for passengers; in fact, had not been used at all for a long time.

"Maybe Hall will be back soon," he said.

Spillane shook his head, and demanded, "Where's your father?"

"San Francisco," Jerry answered, briefly.

Spillane groaned, and fiercely drove his clenched fist into the palm of the other hand. His wife was crying more audibly, and Jerry could hear her murmuring, "And daddy's dyin', dyin'!"

The tears welled up in his own eyes, and he stood irresolute, not knowing what he should do. But the man decided for him.

"Look here, kid," he said, with determination, "the wife and me are goin' over on this here cable of yours! Will you run it for us?"

Jerry backed slightly away. He did it unconsciously, as if recoiling instinctively from something unwelcome.

"Better see if Hall's back," he suggested.

"And if he ain't?"

Again Jerry hesitated.

"I'll stand for the risk," Spillane added. "Don't you see, kid, we've simply got to cross!"

Jerry nodded his head reluctantly.

"And there ain't no use waitin' for Hall," Spillane went on. "You know as well as me he ain't back from Cripple Cow this time of day! So come along and let's get started."

115

No wonder that Mrs. Spillane seemed terrified as they helped her into the ore-car—so Jerry thought, as he gazed into the apparently fathomless gulf beneath her. For it was so filled with rain and cloud, hurtling and curling in the fierce blast, that the other shore, seven hundred feet away, was invisible, while the cliff at their feet dropped sheer down and lost itself in the swirling vapor. By all appearances it might be a mile to bottom instead of two hundred feet.

"All ready?" he asked.

"Let her go!" Spillane shouted, to make himself heard above the roar of the wind.

He had clambered in beside his wife, and was holding one of her hands in his.

Jerry looked upon this with disapproval. "You'll need all your hands for holdin' on, the way the wind's yowlin'."

The man and the woman shifted their hands accordingly, tightly gripping the sides of the car, and Jerry slowly and carefully released the brake. The drum began to revolve as the endless cable passed round it, and the car slid slowly out into the chasm, its trolley wheels rolling on the stationary cable overhead, to which it was suspended.

It was not the first time Jerry had worked the cable, but it was the first time he had done so away from the supervising eye of his father. By means of the brake he regulated the speed of the car. It needed regulating, for at times, caught by the stronger gusts of wind, it swayed violently back and forth; and once, just before it was swallowed up in a rain squall, it seemed about to spill out its human contents.

116

After that Jerry had no way of knowing where the car was except by means of the cable. This he watched keenly as it glided around the drum. "Three hundred feet," he breathed to himself, as the cable markings went by, "three hundred and fifty, four hundred; four hundred and——"

The cable had stopped. Jerry threw off the brake, but it did not move. He caught the cable with his hands and tried to start it by tugging smartly. Something had gone wrong. What? He could not guess; he could not see. Looking up, he could vaguely make out the empty car, which had been crossing from the opposite cliff at a speed equal to that of the loaded car. It was about two hundred and fifty feet away. That meant, he knew, that somewhere in the gray obscurity, two hundred feet above the river and two hundred and fifty feet from the other bank, Spillane and his wife were suspended and stationary.

Three times Jerry shouted with all the shrill force of his lungs, but no answering cry came out of the storm. It was impossible for him to hear them or to make himself heard. As he stood for a moment, thinking rapidly, the flying clouds seemed to thin and lift. He caught a brief glimpse of the swollen Sacramento beneath, and a briefer glimpse of the car and the man and woman. Then the clouds descended thicker than ever.

The boy examined the drum closely, and found nothing the matter with it. Evidently it was the drum on the other side that had gone wrong. He was appalled at the thought of the man and woman out there in the midst of the storm, hanging over the abyss, rocking back and forth in the frail car and ignorant of what was taking place on shore. And he did not like to think of their hanging there while he went round by the Yellow Dragon cable to the other drum.

117

But he remembered a block and tackle in the tool-house, and ran and brought it. They were double blocks, and he murmured aloud, "A purchase of four," as he made the tackle fast to the endless cable. Then he heaved upon it, heaved until it seemed that his arms were being drawn out from their sockets and that his shoulder muscles would be ripped asunder. Yet the cable did not budge. Nothing remained but to cross over to the other side.

He was already soaking wet, so he did not mind the rain as he ran over the trail to the Yellow Dragon. The storm was with him, and it was easy going, although there was no Hall at the other end of it to man the brake for him and regulate the speed of the car. This he did for himself, however, by means of a stout rope, which he passed, with a turn, round the stationary cable.

As the full force of the wind struck him in mid-air, swaying the cable and whistling and roaring past it, and rocking and careening the car, he appreciated more fully what must be the condition of mind of Spillane and his wife. And this appreciation gave strength to him, as, safely across, he fought his way up the other bank, in the teeth of the gale, to the Yellow Dream cable.

To his consternation, he found the drum in thorough working order. Everything was running smoothly at both ends. Where was the hitch? In the middle, without a doubt.

From this side, the car containing Spillane was only two hundred and fifty feet away. He could make out the man and woman through the whirling vapor, crouching in the bottom of the car and exposed to the pelting rain and the full fury of the wind. In a lull between the squalls he shouted to Spillane to examine the trolley of the car.

Spillane heard, for he saw him rise up cautiously on his knees, and with his hands go over both trolley-wheels. Then he turned his face toward the bank.

"She's all right, kid!"

Jerry heard the words, faint and far, as from a remote distance. Then what was the matter? Nothing remained but the other and empty car, which he could not see, but which he knew to be there, somewhere in that terrible gulf two hundred feet beyond Spillane's car.

His mind was made up on the instant. He was only fourteen years old, slightly and wirily built; but his life had been lived among the mountains, his father had taught him no small measure of "sailoring," and he was not particularly afraid of heights.

In the tool-box by the drum he found an old monkey-wrench and a short bar of iron, also a coil of fairly new Manila rope. He looked in vain for a piece of board with which to rig a "boatswain's chair." There was nothing at hand but large planks, which he had no means of sawing, so he was compelled to do without the more comfortable form of saddle.

The saddle he rigged was very simple. With the rope he made merely a large loop round the stationary cable, to which hung the empty car. When he sat in the loop his hands could just reach the cable conveniently, and where the rope was likely to fray against the cable he lashed his coat, in lieu of the old sack he would have used had he been able to find one.

These preparations swiftly completed, he swung out over the chasm, sitting in the rope saddle and pulling himself along the cable by his hands. With him he carried the monkey-wrench and short iron bar and a few spare feet of rope. It was a slightly up-hill pull, but this he did not mind so much as the wind. When the furious gusts hurled him back and forth, sometimes half twisting him about, and he gazed down into the gray depths, he was aware that he was afraid. It was an old cable. What if it should break under his weight and the pressure of the wind?

It was fear he was experiencing, honest fear, and he knew that there was a "gone" feeling in the pit of his stomach, and a trembling of the knees which he could not quell.

But he held himself bravely to the task. The cable was old and worn, sharp pieces of wire projected from it, and his hands were cut and bleeding by the time he took his first rest, and held a shouted conversation with Spillane. The car was directly beneath him and only a few feet away, so he was able to explain the condition of affairs and his errand.

"Wish I could help you," Spillane shouted at him as he started on, "but the wife's gone all to pieces! Anyway, kid, take care of yourself! I got myself in this fix, but it's up to you to get me out!"

"Oh, I'll do it!" Jerry shouted back. "Tell Mrs. Spillane that she'll be ashore now in a jiffy!"

In the midst of pelting rain, which half-blinded him, swinging from side to side like a rapid and erratic pendulum, his torn hands paining him severely and his lungs panting from his exertions and panting from the very air which the wind sometimes blew into his mouth with strangling force, he finally arrived at the empty car.

A single glance showed him that he had not made the dangerous journey in vain. The front trolley-wheel, loose from long wear, had jumped the cable, and the cable was now jammed tightly between the wheel and the sheave-block.

One thing was clear—the wheel must be removed from the block. A second thing was equally clear—while the wheel was being removed the car would have to be fastened to the cable by the rope he had brought.

At the end of a quarter of an hour, beyond making the car secure, he had accomplished nothing. The key which bound the wheel on its axle was rusted and jammed. He hammered at it with one hand and held on the best he could with the other, but the wind persisted in swinging and twisting his body, and made his blows miss more often than not. Nine-tenths of the strength he expended was in trying to hold himself steady. For fear that he might drop the monkey-wrench he made it fast to his wrist with his handkerchief.

At the end of half an hour Jerry had hammered the key clear, but he could not draw it out. A dozen times it seemed that he must give up in despair, that all the danger and toil he had gone through were for nothing. Then an idea came to him, and he went through his pockets with feverish haste, and found what he sought—a ten-penny nail.

But for that nail, put in his pocket he knew not when or why, he would have had to make another trip over the cable and back. Thrusting the nail through the looped head of the key, he at last had a grip, and in no time the key was out.

Then came punching and prying with the iron bar to get the wheel itself free from where it was jammed by the cable against the side of the block. After that Jerry replaced the wheel, and by means of the rope, heaved up on the car till the trolley once more rested properly on the cable.

All this took time. More than an hour and a half had elapsed since his arrival at the empty car. And now, for the first time, he dropped out of his saddle and down into the car. He removed the detaining ropes, and the trolley-wheel began slowly to revolve. The car was moving, and he knew that somewhere beyond, although he could not see, the car of Spillane was likewise moving, and in the opposite direction.

There was no need for a brake, for his weight sufficiently counterbalanced the weight in the other car; and soon he saw the cliff rising out of the cloud depths and the old familiar drum going round and round.

Jerry climbed out and made the car securely fast. He did it deliberately and carefully, and then, quite unhero-like, he sank down by the drum, regardless of the pelting storm, and burst out sobbing.

There were many reasons why he sobbed—partly from the pain of his hand, which was excruciating; partly from exhaustion; partly from relief and release from the nerve-tension he had been under for so long; and in a large measure for thankfulness that the man and woman were saved.

They were not there to thank him; but somewhere beyond that howling, storm-driven gulf he knew they were hurrying over the trail toward the Clover Leaf.

Jerry staggered to the cabin, and his hand left the white knob red with blood as he opened the door, but he took no notice of it.

He was too proudly contented with himself, for he was certain that he had done well, and he was honest enough to admit to himself that he had done well. But a small regret arose and persisted in his thoughts—if his father had only been there to see!

Somewhere along Theater Street he had lost it. He remembered being hustled somewhat roughly on the bridge over one of the canals that cross that busy thoroughfare. Possibly some slant-eyed, light-fingered pickpocket was even then enjoying the fifty-odd yen his purse had contained. And then again, he thought, he might have lost it himself, just lost it carelessly.

Hopelessly, and for the twentieth time, he searched in all his pockets for the missing purse. It was not there. His hand lingered in his empty hip-pocket, and he woefully regarded the voluble and vociferous restaurant-keeper, who insanely clamored: "Twenty-five sen! You pay now! Twenty-five sen!"

"But my purse!" the boy said. "I tell you I've lost it somewhere."

Whereupon the restaurant-keeper lifted his arms indignantly and shrieked: "Twenty-five sen! Twenty-five sen! You pay now!"

Quite a crowd had collected, and it was growing embarrassing for Alf Davis.

It was so ridiculous and petty, Alf thought. Such a disturbance about nothing! And, decidedly, he must be doing something. Thoughts of diving wildly through that forest of legs, and of striking out at whomsoever opposed him, flashed through his mind; but, as though divining his purpose, one of the waiters, a short and chunky chap with an evil-looking cast in one eye, seized him by the arm.

"You pay now! You pay now! Twenty-five sen!" yelled the proprietor, hoarse with rage.

Alf was red in the face, too, from mortification; but he resolutely set out on another exploration. He had given up the purse, pinning his last hope on stray coins. In the little change-pocket of his coat he found a ten-sen piece and five-copper sen; and remembering having recently missed a ten-sen piece, he cut the seam of the pocket and resurrected the coin from the depths of the lining. Twenty-five sen he held in his hand, the sum required to pay for the supper he had eaten. He turned them over to the proprietor, who counted them, grew suddenly calm, and bowed obsequiously—in fact, the whole crowd bowed obsequiously and melted away.

Alf Davis was a young sailor, just turned sixteen, on board the Annie Mine, an American sailing-schooner, which had run into Yokohama to ship its season's catch of skins to London. And in this, his second trip ashore, he was beginning to snatch his first puzzling glimpses of the Oriental mind. He laughed when the bowing and kotowing was over, and turned on his heel to confront another problem. How was he to get aboard ship? It was eleven o'clock at night, and there would be no ship's boats ashore, while the outlook for hiring a native boatman, with nothing but empty pockets to draw upon, was not particularly inviting.

Keeping a sharp lookout for shipmates, he went down to the pier. At Yokohama there are no long lines of wharves. The shipping lies out at anchor, enabling a few hundred of the short-legged people to make a livelihood by carrying passengers to and from the shore.

A dozen sampan men and boys hailed Alf and offered their services. He selected the most favorable-looking one, an old and beneficent-appearing man with a withered leg. Alf stepped into his sampan and sat down. It was quite dark and he could not see what the old fellow was doing, though he evidently was doing nothing

124

about shoving off and getting under way. At last he limped over and peered into Alf's face.

"Ten sen," he said.

"Yes, I know, ten sen," Alf answered carelessly. "But hurry up. American schooner."

"Ten sen. You pay now," the old fellow insisted.

Alf felt himself grow hot all over at the hateful words "pay now." "You take me to American schooner; then I pay," he said.

But the man stood up patiently before him, held out his hand, and said, "Ten sen. You pay now."

Alf tried to explain. He had no money. He had lost his purse. But he would pay. As soon as he got aboard the American schooner, then he would pay. No; he would not even go aboard the American schooner. He would call to his shipmates, and they would give the sampan man the ten sen first. After that he would go aboard. So it was all right, of course.

To all of which the beneficent-appearing old man replied: "You pay now. Ten sen." And, to make matters worse, the other sampan men squatted on the pier steps, listening.

Alf, chagrined and angry, stood up to step ashore. But the old fellow laid a detaining hand on his sleeve. "You give shirt now. I take you 'Merican schooner," he proposed.

Then it was that all of Alf's American independence flamed up in his breast. The Anglo-Saxon has a born dislike of being imposed upon, and to Alf this was sheer robbery! Ten sen was equivalent to six American cents, while his shirt, which was of good quality and was new, had cost him two dollars.

125

He turned his back on the man without a word, and went out to the end of the pier, the crowd, laughing with great gusto, following at his heels. The majority of them were heavy-set, muscular fellows, and the July night being one of sweltering heat, they were clad in the least possible raiment. The water-people of any race are rough and turbulent, and it struck Alf that to be out at midnight on a pier-end with such a crowd of wharfmen, in a big Japanese city, was not as safe as it might be.

One burly fellow, with a shock of black hair and ferocious eyes, came up. The rest shoved in after him to take part in the discussion.

"Give me shoes," the man said. "Give me shoes now. I take you 'Merican schooner."

Alf shook his head, whereat the crowd clamored that he accept the proposal. Now the Anglo-Saxon is so constituted that to browbeat or bully him is the last way under the sun of getting him to do any certain thing. He will dare willingly, but he will not permit himself to be driven. So this attempt of the boatmen to force Alf only aroused all the dogged stubbornness of his race. The same qualities were in him that are in men who lead forlorn hopes; and there, under the stars, on the lonely pier, encircled by the jostling and shouldering gang, he resolved that he would die rather than submit to the indignity of being robbed of a single stitch of clothing. Not value, but principle, was at stake.

Then somebody thrust roughly against him from behind. He whirled about with flashing eyes, and the circle involuntarily gave ground. But the crowd was growing more boisterous. Each and every article of clothing he had on was demanded by one or another, and these demands were shouted simultaneously at the tops of very healthy lungs.

126

Alf had long since ceased to say anything, but he knew that the situation was getting dangerous, and that the only thing left to him was to get away. His face was set doggedly, his eyes glinted like points of steel, and his body was firmly and confidently poised. This air of determination sufficiently impressed the boatmen to make them give way before him When he started to walk toward the shore-end of the pier. But they trooped along beside more noisily than ever. One of the youngsters about Alf's size and build, impudently snatched his cap from his head; and before he could put it on his own head, Alf struck out from the shoulder, and sent the fellow rolling on the stones.

The cap flew out of his hand and disappeared among the many legs. Alf did some quick thinking, his sailor pride would not permit him to leave the cap in their hands. He followed in the direction it had sped, and soon found it under the bare foot of a stalwart fellow, who kept his weight stolidly upon it. Alf tried to get the cap by a sudden jerk, but failed. He shoved against the man's leg, but the man only grunted. It was challenge direct, and Alf accepted it. Like a flash one leg was behind the man and Alf had thrust strongly with his shoulder against the fellow's chest. Nothing could save the man from the fierce vigorousness of the trick, and he was hurled over and backward.

Next, the cap was on Alf's head and his fists were up before him. Then he whirled about to prevent attack from behind, and all those in that quarter fled precipitately. This was what he wanted. None remained between him and the shore end. The pier was narrow. Facing them and threatening with his fist those who attempted to pass him on either side, he continued his retreat. It was exciting work, walking backward and at the same time checking that surging mass of men. But the dark-skinned peoples, the world over, have learned to respect the white man's fist; and it was the battles fought by many sailors, more than his own warlike front, that gave Alf the victory.

Where the pier adjoins the shore was the station of the harbor police, and Alf backed into the electric-lighted office, very much to the amusement of the dapper lieutenant in charge. The sampan men, grown quiet and orderly, clustered like flies by the open door, through which they could see and hear what passed.

Alf explained his difficulty in few words, and demanded, as the privilege of a stranger in a strange land, that the lieutenant put him aboard in the police-boat. The lieutenant, in turn, who knew all the "rules and regulations" by heart, explained that the harbor police were not ferrymen, and that the police-boats had other functions to perform than that of transporting belated and penniless sailormen to their ships. He also said he knew the sampan men to be natural-born robbers, but that so long as they robbed within the law he was powerless. It was their right to collect fares in advance, and who was he to command them to take a passenger and collect fare at the journey's end? Alf acknowledged the justice of his remarks, but suggested that while he could not command he might persuade. The lieutenant was willing to oblige, and went to the door, from where he delivered a speech to the crowd. But they, too, knew their rights, and, when the officer had finished, shouted in chorus their abominable "Ten sen! You pay now! You pay now!"

"You see, I can do nothing," said the lieutenant, who, by the way, spoke perfect English. "But I have warned them not to harm or molest you, so you will be safe, at least. The night is warm and half over. Lie down somewhere and go to sleep. I would permit you to sleep here in the office, were it not against the rules and regulations."

Alf thanked him for his kindness and courtesy; but the sampan men had aroused all his pride of race and doggedness, and the problem could not be solved that way. To sleep out the night on the stones was an acknowledgment of defeat.

"The sampan men refuse to take me out?"

The lieutenant nodded.

"And you refuse to take me out?"

Again the lieutenant nodded.

"Well, then, it's not in the rules and regulations that you can prevent my taking myself out?"

The lieutenant was perplexed. "There is no boat," he said.

"That's not the question," Alf proclaimed hotly. "If I take myself out, everybody's satisfied and no harm done?"

"Yes; what you say is true," persisted the puzzled lieutenant. "But you cannot take yourself out."

"You just watch me," was the retort.

Down went Alf's cap on the office floor. Right and left he kicked off his low-cut shoes. Trousers and shirt followed.

"Remember," he said in ringing tones, "I, as a citizen of the United States, shall hold you, the city of Yokohama, and the government of Japan responsible for those clothes. Good night."

He plunged through the doorway, scattering the astounded boatmen to either side, and ran out on the pier. But they quickly recovered and ran after him, shouting with glee at the new phase the situation had taken on. It was a night long remembered among the water-folk of Yokohama town. Straight to the end Alf ran, and, without pause, dived off cleanly and neatly into the water. He struck out with a lusty, single-overhand stroke till curiosity prompted him to halt for a moment. Out of the darkness, from where the pier should be, voices were calling to him.

He turned on his back, floated, and listened.

"All right! All right!" he could distinguish from the babel. "No pay now; pay bime by! Come back! Come back now; pay bime by!"

"No, thank you," he called back. "No pay at all. Good night."

Then he faced about in order to locate the Annie Mine. She was fully a mile away, and in the darkness it was no easy task to get her bearings. First, he settled upon a blaze of lights which he knew nothing but a man-of-war could make. That must be the United States war-ship Lancaster. Somewhere to the left and beyond should be the Annie Mine. But to the left he made out three lights close together. That could not be the schooner. For the moment he was confused. He rolled over on his back and shut his eyes, striving to construct a mental picture of the harbor as he had seen it in daytime. With a snort of satisfaction he rolled back again. The three lights evidently belonged to the big English tramp steamer. Therefore the schooner must lie somewhere between the three lights and the Lancaster. He gazed long and steadily, and there, very dim and low, but at the point he expected, burned a single light—the anchor-light of the Annie Mine.

And it was a fine swim under the starshine. The air was warm as the water, and the water as warm as tepid milk. The good salt taste of it was in his mouth, the tingling of it along his limbs; and the steady beat of his heart, heavy and strong, made him glad for living.

But beyond being glorious the swim was uneventful. On the right hand he passed the many-lighted Lancaster, on the left hand the English tramp, and ere long the Annie Mine loomed large above him. He grasped the hanging rope-ladder and drew himself noiselessly on deck. There was no one in sight. He saw a light in the galley, and knew that the captain's son, who kept the lonely anchor-watch, was making coffee. Alf went forward to the forecastle. The men were snoring in their bunks, and in that confined space the heat seemed to him insufferable. So he put on a thin cotton shirt and a pair of dungaree trousers, tucked blanket and pillow under his arm, and went up on deck and out on the forecastle-head.

Hardly had he begun to doze when he was roused by a boat coming alongside and hailing the anchor-watch. It was the police-boat, and to Alf it was given to enjoy the excited conversation that ensued. Yes, the captain's son recognized the clothes. They belonged to Alf Davis, one of the seamen. What had happened? No; Alf Davis had not come aboard. He was ashore. He was not ashore? Then he must be drowned. Here both the lieutenant and the captain's son talked at the same time, and Alf could make out nothing. Then he heard them come forward and rouse out the crew. The crew grumbled sleepily and said that Alf Davis was not in the forecastle; whereupon the captain's son waxed indignant at the Yokohama police and their ways, and the lieutenant quoted rules and regulations in despairing accents.

Alf rose up from the forecastle-head and extended his hand, saying:

"I guess I'll take those clothes. Thank you for bringing them aboard so promptly."

131

"I don't see why he couldn't have brought you aboard inside of them," said the captain's son.

And the police lieutenant said nothing, though he turned the clothes over somewhat sheepishly to their rightful owner.

The next day, when Alf started to go ashore, he found himself surrounded by shouting and gesticulating, though very respectful, sampan men, all extraordinarily anxious to have him for a passenger. Nor did the one he selected say, "You pay now," when he entered his boat. When Alf prepared to step out on to the pier, he offered the man the customary ten sen. But the man drew himself up and shook his head.

"You all right," he said. "You no pay. You never no pay. You bully boy and all right."

And for the rest of the Annie Mine's stay in port, the sampan men refused money at Alf Davis's hand. Out of admiration for his pluck and independence, they had given him the freedom of the harbor.